IMPOSSIBILITY!

Dake instinctively lifted his hand to touch his face.
He rubbed his left cheek with his right hand. It felt
completely normal. He ran his hand across his mouth
and suddenly stopped, his heart thudding. He gingerly touched his right cheek, his fingertips making
a whispering sound against the hard, polished bone.
He touched the empty ivory eye socket . . .

Impossible!—yet there in the mirror was the half
death's head staring back at him. The illusion of a
diseased mind? No. Dake knew the answer, but how
could he convince the rest of mankind of the unbe-
lievable truth?

*Master storyteller JOHN D. MACDONALD takes to
the literature of the imagination to produce a
spellbinding tale of human strength in the face of
ultimate paradox.*

BALLROOM
OF THE SKIES

John D. MacDonald

A FAWCETT GOLD MEDAL BOOK

Fawcett Publications, Inc., Greenwich, Conn.

No question is so difficult to answer as that to which the answer is obvious.

—GEORGE BERNARD SHAW

CHAPTER ONE

The world, Branson thought, is like that circus act of long ago, back in the sweet-colored days of childhood, when the big top was as high as the sky, and gigantic horses marched the earth.

He remembered the act. The ragged clown teetering on the high wire, clutching his misshapen hat, reeling toward destruction, catching himself in that last throat-thickening instant to flounder some more. You believed in him then. That poor dazed clown, petrified by height, yet trying with pathetic and humble courage to please the crowd, taking from the baggy clothes the white dinner plates and, fighting his fear and his constant losses of balance, managing somehow to juggle the plates. Oh, how white they had shined in the spotlights!

You could see how the awkward body would plummet to the hard earth, and you wanted to stop looking, yet could not stop. And then suddenly his balance became sure and certain. He stripped off the baggy clothes to reveal himself, taut and muscular in the spangled tights, bowing to applause. You laughed aloud into Daddy's eyes, knowing how close you had been to tears.

Now all the men of the world watched the humble clown on the high wire. He juggled atomics, and napalm and all the hundred ways to separate the soul from the body, either quickly or very slowly. He wavered up there in the spotlights and all the eyes watched, knowing that when at last he fell, it would all be gone—the tent and the music and the elephant girls, forever and ever. He had remained up there too long. The nerves of men were ground thin and fine. You waited for him to strip off the baggy

clown clothes and bow to the applause of the world. But
he never did. He was caught up there, impaled for eternity
on the bright shafts of the spotlights.

Once he had seen a revival of a Harold Lloyd picture. He
had seen it when he was a child, at the Museum of Modern Art, and the picture, even then, had been fifty years
old. The bespectacled man had been blindfolded and he
was walking about in the steel beams of a building under
construction, a skyscraper, back in the days when buildings stretched upward toward the sun, rather than down-
ward into the warm safe earth.

The comedian had not known he was a dizzy height in
the air. He wandered about aimlessly, arms outstretched.
When he stepped off into space a girder, being hoisted up
from below, would always present itself just in time to
take his weight. It had been one of those Saturday showings. He remembered how all the children had screamed at
the tension of that old silent film.

Maybe it was a truer analogy, because the clown was
aware of his danger, and the comedian walked in an absurd innocence.

Now the Museum of Modern Art was gone, and the
dwindling radiation of the area was so slight that the lead
sheaths on the buses were more to impress the tourists
than from any real necessity.

That had been the time, in the early seventies, when you
had been certain that the clown would fall, that the beam
would not arrive in time. But they had pocked one another's cities with the new ugliness, hurled the dwindling
wealth of the planet at each other for a time. Ostensibly
the democracies had won. The armies had hammered their
way back and forth across Europe for the third and last
time. Now, as had been predicted so many times before,
Europe was wasteland, physically and spiritually incapable
ot rising again from her knees. Vassal states, with marginal resources, struggling for meager existence.

Somehow, insanely, the world had caught itself once
more—saved itself on the very brink of destruction. Ot all
the industrial economies left, only Pak-India, reunited,
was capable of trying again. And India wasn't interested.

The astonishing effect on her standard of living as a result of the ruthless years of compulsory sterilization had given her the vigor to absorb Burma, Thailand, Ceylon, the Malay Peninsula and a rich slice of south China. Reclamation of jungle and desert gave her the most solid basis of raw materials in the world, with the exception, perhaps, of Brazil, which had but recently moved her seat of government to Buenos Aires.

It wasn't, Branson thought, the line-up that anyone could have guessed back in the days before the war. Communism, both as a religion and as a political theory, had failed when its pie in the sky hadn't materialized. It had failed when it had run up against man's peculiarly basic desire to do as he damn pleased.

Each time the world tottered on the high wire, it recovered its balance in a weird and wonderful way. Now Pak-India was the king-pin democracy, with the United States trying to assure itself that it was a full partner, rather than, as was obvious to any objective person, a junior partner. Huddled together under India's skirts were all of the nations of Europe except Spain—all the nations, including those new nations which were the result of a partitioned Russia. Also, under the same skirt, was Australia, Canada.

But the clock had turned backward and the new enemy was the old enemy all over again. Fascism—a strong triple coalition of Brazil, which had taken over three quarters of the South American continent, marching and singing under the silver banners of Garva, and North China, singing the same songs, though with oriental dissonance, under a man called Stephen Chu, and Irania, which included Arabia, Egypt, most of North Africa marching with burnoose and iron heels under the guidance of that renegade Anglo-Egyptian, George Fahdi.

The crazy years since the war had passed, and now all the strong new lines were drawn. Don't step over my line. Look at my armies, my bomber fleets, my missile stations. Don't step over my line.

Malthus would have called the war a failure. It killed only seven millions. And each day, Branson knew, eighty thousand new souls and mouths were added to the world.

Eighty thousand net. Nearly thirty millions a year. The old ant-heap pressure, leaning on us again. The eighty thousand increment each day was a jackstraw to be placed carefully on a precarious structure. Use steady hands, there. You aren't building it right. Build it my way. Build it my way, or else. . . .

The Fourth World War coming in from the deeps, rolling up in an oily way, ready to crest and smash on what was left of the world. And now, each time, it had to be the last one. Yet, somehow, it never was.

The clown world fought for balance. The comedian stepped off into space.

Branson left his desk and walked over to the window. Rent cheaply and in fear, and you get a window to look out of. An expensive office would have a clever diorama where the window would be. The psychologists had become important to underground architecture. If a man must live and work underground, it must be made to look like above-ground, because man is not a mole.

In the bright noisy dusk of New Times Square, ten stories below, the crowds moved slowly. American cars wheezed and clattered through the streets, their turbines laboring under the low-grade fuels. Here and there he could see a long glittering Taj or a Brahma, cars whose cost and upkeep were far beyond the purse of anyone who worked for wages. The Indians made the best automobiles in the world. Tata Automotive designed cars for looks and power, while what was left of Detroit had to concentrate on substitute materials, on fuel economy, on standardization of design from year to year. Some of the foreign cars, he knew, would be driven by tourists from Pak-India. It was sometimes difficult to stomach their arrogance, their conscious certainty that everything in India was better than here in the States. Far better. They had, somehow, become the brash new nation, the young giant born in ashes, rising to strength.

But, Branson knew, they had to be dealt with delicately. Their tourist rupees were sadly needed. And their embassies were powerful. Odd how, if you didn't speak either Hindi or Tamil, they thought they could make you understand by yelling at you. Their President, Gondohl Lahl, had that same arrogance. The only product of America which India seemed to approve of wholeheartedly was the beauty of its longlegged girls.

Some of the weariness of the past year left Darwin Branson as he thought that it was barely conceivable that now, through his own efforts, the war-tide might be halted, the drums and bugles stilled. His mission had been a secret one, entrusted to him by that wise, farsighted President of the United States, Robert Enfield. From the practical point of view, it had merely been a piece of horsetrading. Enfield, and the other leaders, had known that the economy could not stand another war. India could get nowhere by demanding, and she refused to plead. The triple coalition would not deal with India directly on these matters. The United States became the *sub rosa* contact between them.

What Darwin Branson had seen in Buenos Aires, in Alexandria, in Shanghai, in Bombay, had convinced him, all over again, that the nature of man is good, rather than evil. There was fear all over the world. Now, at last, the era of the man of good will could be initiated.

It had been a hole and corner affair. Meetings in furtive places, in cheap offices such as this one. Two more meetings and the deal could be made. A new mutual assistance pact for the world at large. Something, at last, with meaning. Something that would unwind the hard strands of fear and give mankind breathing space again, give him time to look around.

He looked at his watch. Another twenty minutes of thought, of solitude, and they would join him. Young Dake Lorin who had been his assistant, his husky right arm during the long year of cautious dickering. And that strange Englishman, Smith, who was empowered by his Leader, George Fahdi, to make a deal. Once all the offers were in, President Gondohl Lahl could be contacted. See the concessions the others will make? And this is all they want from you. The net result will be a bettering of the standard of living in every nation involved. And that will mean an easing of the tension. He had it on good authority

that Gondohl Lahl would go along with it, and he knew
that Smith would be cooperative.

He stood at the window, a small tired man with white
hair and a furrowed face, eyes with a look of kindness.
Midwife to peace. That was what Robert had called him.

Fifteen more minutes. He heard footsteps in the empty
corridor. Thinking they had arrived earlier than planned,
he went to the door and opened it. The young couple
seemed unremarkable. They had better than average
looks, and a disconcertingly assured way.

"I'm afraid you have the wrong office," Darwin Branson said politely.

"I'm afraid we have the right one, sir," the young man
said, almost regretfully. There was always the danger of
assassination by fanatics. Yet this couple did not have that
special look, unmistakable once seen.

Darwin Branson was still pondering that point when the
young man killed him, so quickly, with such an astounding
speed that there was no interval between life and death, no
period wherein Darwin Branson was permitted to be
aware that life had gone and the great darkness had
begun.

The girl caught the body, carried it lightly and easily
into the alcove. She stood, holding the body, her face
expressionless, while her companion made quick prepara-
tions. The hand tool made a faint electronic whirr. She
placed the body on the screen he had unfolded. She
walked out of the alcove and stood waiting. She heard the
water running in the alcove sink. After a time the whirring
stopped, and then the sound of water. Her companion
came out, refolding the screen. He nodded and she went to
the office door, opened it. Darwin Branson stood outside,
his face as empty as death. She motioned to him. He
walked in woodenly and took his seat behind the desk.
The man leaned over and whispered one word into Darwin Branson's ear. He nodded to the girl and they went
out of the office, closed the door.

"Thirty seconds," the girl said. The man knocked on
the office door. Darwin Branson came to the door.

"I'm afraid you have the wrong office," Darwin Branson said politely.

The young man smiled. "Sorry, sir. I guess I have. Pardon me for bothering you."

"Perfectly all right," Branson said. The couple walked to the stairs. They went down five stairs and waited. They heard the elevator come up, stop. The door clanged open. Two men walked toward Branson's office.

The man nodded at the girl. She responded with a quick, almost shy smile. It was full night. He opened the stairwell window and they stepped easily out onto the narrow sill above the street. He closed the window behind them. They reappeared in the same instant on the high cornice of a building across the square. They looked down into the lighted office below, where three men were talking earnestly. Then the couple played a wild game, flickering like black flames from one high stone shoulder to the next, until at last he seemed to guess her intent and appeared at the same instant she did on the splintered stub of the Statue of Liberty in the harbor, touched her shoulder before she could escape. They laughed silently. It had been like the crazy game of children who had finished a hard lesson. They clasped hands and were gone.

Back in the office Darwin Branson talked to Smith. He instinctively did not like the man, did not trust him. Smith had . . . an oily look, a slippery look. Perhaps it would not be wise to trust him with the whole picture. He looked as though he could twist it this way and that, turn it inside out and find there some advantage for himself.

Dake Lorin sat, apparently taken in by Smith. Darwin Branson felt a bit contemptuous toward Dake Lorin. That young man was so . . . excessively noble. So naive and gullible. Dake would have you believe that the world could become a Garden of Eden once again. Sitting there, the whole preposterous six feet six inches of him, with that harsh black hair, and the dumb shelf of brow over the shadowed eyes, giving his face a simian look, as though Dake were some great sad ape trying mournfully to rectify

the errors of mankind. Dake was just the type to be taken
in by this oily Smith person.

As Darwin Branson talked he wondered why he had
wasted the past year on this chase of the wild goose. A few
compromises would make no difference. The world was
war bound, and Robert Enfield should stop kidding himself, stop thinking that the United States could step in with
sub rosa mediation and stave off disaster. The crucial
point, rather, was to select the winning side while there
was still time to make a selection.

He saw that Smith was aware of his contempt, and he
was amused.

CHAPTER TWO

Smith had been awkwardly skeptical. He was a moon-
faced man with nail-head eyes, fat babyish hands. Dake
Lorin had exerted himself to be charming, to make a
friend of this Smith. It had been most difficult. He kept
thinking that Smith was a complicated mechanical doll.
And if you tripped the wrong reflex, you would be inun-
dated by the standard line. Irania is strong. Irania is quick.
Irania is brave. Our leader, George Fahdi, is farsighted.

Smith was in the country on a forged passport, arranged
with the oblique assistance of one of the Under Secretaries
of State. Dake had picked him up in Boston to drive him
down to the conference with Darwin Branson.

The trick was to get under the automatic pseudo-pa-
triotic reflex, and get down to the man himself.

Dake drove the small nondescript car at a sedate sixty-
five, slowing for the stretches of neglected shattered
slabs. The car, like most of the works of man, was a shade
too small for Dake Lorin. His knees and elbows seemed
always to be in the way.

"I understand your Leader was impressed with Mr.
Branson."

Smith shrugged. "He told me later that he felt Mr.
Branson was a great rarity. A good man. There are not
many good men."

"I've worked with Mr. Branson for a year."

Smith turned in the seat. "So? You are . . . by trade, a
government employee?"

"Not by trade. By trade I guess I'm a newspaperman. I
was filling in in the Washington Bureau a couple of years

15

ago. I interviewed Branson. He . . . stuck with me. The
guy has quite an effect."

"You intrigue me," Smith said in his toneless voice.

Dake made a small decision. In order to disarm this
Smith he would have to do a bit of a striptease, let his
soul show a bit. "I've always been a lone wolf type, Mr.
Smith. Maybe a bit of a visionary. That state of mind always had a cause, I suppose. When I was twelve, a wide-
eyed kid, the police picked up my Dad. He was a small-
time politician. And a thief. He would have been safe all
his life, but there was a change of administration and they
threw him to the wolves. It was a deal. He was supposed
to get eighteen months. But the judge crossed them up and
Dad got ten years. When he found out that his old pal, the
governor, wasn't going to pardon him, he hung himself in
his cell. My mother pulled herself together and we got
along, somehow. I had a lot of schoolyard scraps. It
made a mark on me, I guess. I grew up with a chip on my
shoulder, and a fat urge to change the world so that things
like that couldn't happen."

"Quite a dream to have."

"I suppose so. Anyway, it gave me a drive. I learned the
hard way that I couldn't change the world by punching it
in the mouth. So I decided to instruct the world. I became
a two-bit messiah in the newspaper game. But that's like
knocking down stone walls with your head. What you tell
them on Tuesday they can't remember on Wednesday.
Then I interviewed Darwin Branson and later it seemed as
if he'd been interviewing me. For the first time I'd found a
man I could talk to. A man who believed—just as I believe—in the innate decency of mankind. I talked my fool
head off. And went back, unofficially, to talk some more.
Then, when I heard he was going to retire, I felt lost. As
though the one sane man left in the world had given up.
He got in touch with me and put his new assignment on
the line. I got out of newspaper work right then. And
we've been working on it for a year."

"And it's still a dream, Mr. Lorin?"

"I'll have to let Mr. Branson tell you about that."

"It has been my experience, Mr. Lorin, that visionary

tactics do not fit the world of practical international politics."

"Look at it this way, Mr. Smith. We've been carrying a double load of fear ever since Hiroshima. Every one of us. It has an effect on every joint human action, from marriage to treaties. Fear makes each nation, each combination of nations, aggressive. And that aggressive outlook adds to the increment of fear. Each power group has established 'talking points.' Thus, everyone has demands to make, demands that will apparently not be met."

"We demand that Pak-India cease acts of aggression on their northwest frontier."

"Precisely. And it seems that all the demands balance out. In other words, if, through one vast treaty agreement, all the 'talking points' could be eliminated, it would give us the breathing space we need and . . . it might lead to the habit of similar world treaties in the future, once a new set of demands and 'talking points' have been set up. The result may be visionary. The method is practical, Mr. Smith."

"We will not make concessions," Smith said firmly.

"Stop talking like your Leader, Mr. Smith. Forgive my bluntness. Talk as a man. A living, thinking organism. You have ambition. Otherwise you would not have reached such a high place under George Fahdi. Being in a high place, you sense the precariousness of your position. What would you give to be able to look ten years into the future and see yourself still important, still trusted, still . . . safe?"

"Life is not that certain."

"Yet we all want it to be that certain. We want to know that we will be free to live, and love, and be happy. Yet, as nations, we act in such a way that it increases rather than reduces our uncertainty. As though we were under some compulsion. Like lemmings, racing to the sea to drown themselves. Mr. Branson does not believe that it is necessary that, through our acts as nations, we must live in fear. He believes that, acting as nations, acting in good will, we can make this world as good a place to live as it was during the first fourteen years of this century. Your

Leader is a man, just as you are. As I am. He does not need aggression to consolidate his position. He needs a constantly increasing standard of living to make his place secure. Proper treaties, proper utilization of world resources, can make that possible."

"You sound like a free trader from the history books."

"Perhaps. I am not as convincing as Mr. Branson."

"War, Mr. Lorin, is a cyclical phenomenon."

"That's been our traditional excuse. It's a cycle. Who can stop cycles? It's sunspots. Who can change the sun? Mr. Branson calls that statistical rationalization."

"Your Mr. Branson sounds like an impressive man."

"He is. Believe me, he is."

Dake parked the car in a garage near New Times Square and they walked through the last faint grayness of dusk toward the rented office. Dake was dismally aware that if Smith wished to apply the trite fascist tag of decadent democracy, New Times Square gave him overpowering opportunity. There was no use telling a man like Smith that what he was seeing was a fringe world, a place of fetid lunacies, not at all typical of the heartland of the country where stubborn, dogged men were working in lab and field and mine to re-create, through substitution, the lost wealth of a great nation. The problem of the world, as Branson had said so many times, was in the field of bionomics. Man has made his environment precarious for himself, by denuding it of what he needs. This problem of mankind, the great and pressing problem, is to readjust that environment to make it once more a place where man can exist. Human nature, Branson maintained stoutly, does not have to be changed. It is basically good. Evil acts are the products of fear, uncertainty, insecurity.

The war of the seventies had caused a further moral deterioration. Man sought escape in orgy, in soul-deadening drugs, in curious sadisms. Along 165th Street the fleng joints were in full cry. In the mouth of an alley three women, loaded to the gills with prono, were mercilessly beating a Japanese sailor. Giggling couples pushed their way into a dingy triditorium to rent the shoddy private rooms where the three gleaming curved walls were three-dimensional screens for a life-size, third-rate showing of one of the obscene feature shows turned out in the listless Hollywood mill. Censorship restricted such public showings to heterosexual motifs, but further uptown, private triditoriums showed imported specialties that would gag a gnu.

The land was full of sects which, in revulsion at the metropolitan moralities, had founded new religions that insisted on complete celibacy among the fanatic congregations, each member pledged never to reproduce his kind. A chanting line wearing purple neon halos picketed the triditorium. A child lay dead in the gutter and a haughty Indian stood beside his glistening Taj answering the questions of a servile traffic policeman in a bored and impatient voice.

"In here, Mr. Smith," Dake said, glad to get the man off the street.

They rode up in the groaning elevator, and walked down the hall to the office. Darwin Branson got up quickly from behind his desk. Dake felt a warm assurance at seeing the man, felt an end to his own doubts.

The conference began. Dake was so accustomed to hearing the gentle assurance with which Branson wheedled that he listened with half an ear. He suddenly focused his full, shocked attention on Darwin Branson when he heard him say, a bit coldly, "Naturally, if all the arrangements please your Leader, President Enfield wishes your Leader to . . . ah . . . remember us with friendliness."

Dake said, "Darwin! Good Lord, that implies that we're. . . ."

"Please!" Branson said with soft authority. Dake became reluctantly silent, telling himself that Branson had some good motive for handling this interview on a different tone and level than all the others.

Smith smiled. "I was afraid, after listening to your young friend, Mr. Branson, that I would find myself dealing with a saint. I am glad to detect a . . . shall we say . . . practical approach."

"This country, Mr. Smith, can't afford *not* to make friends, particularly with a coalition as powerful as yours."

"Could I safely say then, that those concessions we make shall be more . . . ah . . . spectacular than effective?"

Dake had never seen quite that smile on Darwin Branson's face before. "Please, Mr. Smith. You must remember that we are gentlemen of sincerity and integrity. Think how President Gondohl Lahl would be annoyed should he begin to think that whereas his concessions were made honestly, yours were made with a view to appearances."

Smith nodded. "I see what you mean. We must, above all else, be sincere. Now I am wondering if . . . your other dealings, with Garva and with Chu, have been made with this same degree of sincerity. I think that is a fair question."

"Of course, Mr. Smith. I will say this. They are all hoping that it is not . . . too good to be true."

"I believe," said Smith, "that I shall offer an alternate concession to the one you ask for. I believe we shall surrender Gibraltar to Spain."

"Eyewash," Dake said hotly. "That means nothing. You can have missile stations zeroed in on it to immunize it any instant you feel like it."

Smith looked at Branson and raised one eyebrow. Branson said, "Don't underestimate his offer, Dake."

"But it's so obvious. You've said a hundred times, Darwin, that each concession has to be real and honest, or the whole thing will fall down. When everyone else sees that Irania is just making a . . . pointless gesture instead of a real concession, they'll withdraw their promises and we'll be back where we were."

"Your young man seems to be filled with childish faith, Mr. Branson."

"An attribute of most young men, I'm afraid. I'll relay your offer to the others, Mr. Smith."

"And spoil a year's work, Darwin," Dake said dully. "I . . . just don't understand."

Branson stood up. "Can we assist you further, Mr. Smith?"

"No thank you. Arrangements have been made for me.

I'll be in Alexandria in the morning. And, I assure you, the Leader will not forget your . . . cooperation."

Smith bowed first to Branson and then, a bit mockingly, to Dake Lorin. He left quietly.

The moment the door shut, Dake said, "You've blown it, Darwin. You've blown it sky-high."

Branson leaned back. He looked weary, but satisfied. "I think I've handled it in the only possible way, Dake. It has become increasingly obvious to me that we couldn't ever bring them all together."

"But yesterday you said . . ."

"Things have happened between yesterday and now. Things I can't explain to you. We've had to lower our sights, Dake. That Smith is an oily specimen, isn't he? But he's the representative of Irania. Oil reserves, Dake. A tremendous backlog of manpower. And influence gradually extending down into Africa, down into vast resources. They'll be good friends, Dake. Good friends to have."

"Now slow up just a minute. That is the kind of thinking, Darwin, we have both openly said we detest. Opportunistic, blind thinking. Lining up with the outfit which seems to have the biggest muscles. Damn it all, this is an about-face which I can't comprehend."

"When one plan looks as if it will fail, you pick the next best. That's mature thinking, Dake."

"Nuts, my friend. It's an evidence of a desire to commit suicide. You, of all the people in the world, to suddenly turn out to be . . ."

"Watch it, Dake!"

"I won't watch it. I gave a year of my life to this, and now I find that all along you've been giving me the big one-world yak, and the brotherhood of man yak, while without letting me know you've been setting us up for a power deal."

"A power deal, my young friend, is the best that an indigent nation can hope for. We have to line up with the people who can hit the quickest and the hardest. I . . . think we've managed it."

"You've managed it. Leave me out of it. I'm through, Darwin. You've tried your best to drag me into it, to as-

sume that somehow—merely through being here with you
—I become some kind of . . . partner. It was more than a
dream, for God's sake!"

"Remember how the British survived for so long, Dake,
after they'd lost their muscles? Always creating that delicate balance of power and . . ."

"Ending in hell, Darwin, when the Indians threw them
out of Fiji, when all the throats in the Solomons were cut.
I can't seem to get through to you. We weren't doing this
for us. We were doing it for the world at large, Darwin."

"Sometimes it is wise to accept half a loaf."

Dake Lorin felt the tingling tension in all his muscles,
felt the uprush of the black crazy anger that was his greatest curse. The blindness came, and he was unaware of his
movements, unaware of time—aware only that he had
somehow reached across the desk to grab the front of
Branson's neat dark suit in one huge fist, had lifted the
smaller man up out of the chair. He shook him until the
face was blurred in his vision.

"Dake!" the man yelled. "Dake!"

The anger slowly receded. He dropped Branson back
into the chair. He felt weak and he was sweating.

"Sorry," he said.

"You're a madman, Lorin!"

"You're a cheap little man, Branson. I have a hunch. I
have the feeling there are people who'll understand exactly
how you sold out the human race on this deal. And I'm
going to put the case before them. All of it. Every part of
it. Then let the world judge you, Branson."

"Now just a moment. This involves a question of security, Lorin. I can have you classified as potentially subver-
sive, have you sent to labor camp until you cool off. You
know that."

"I don't think you can stop me."

"You've been engaged in secret negotiations. Any viola-
tion of security will be evidence of your disloyalty."

Dake said softly, "And you're the man who called those
regulations, called the labor camps, the new barbarism,
government by aboriginal decree. You changed overnight,

Darwin. You're not the same man. I'll do what I can, and you can kindly go to hell."

"While you're doing it, examine your own motives again, Dake. Maybe you've spent your life looking for martyrdom, and this is your best opportunity."

"That's a low blow."

"You're upset, Dake. In a way I don't blame you. Disappointment is hard to take. But you are my friend. I don't want to see you hurt."

Dake stared at him for long seconds. There was nothing else to say. He turned on his heel and left the office, slamming the door violently behind him, taking wry pleasure in the childishness of the gesture.

CHAPTER THREE

In the stately cathedral hush of the austere Times-News offices the following morning, Dake Lorin was slowly and uneasily passed up the ladder from managing editor to assistant publisher, to publisher. He sat in paneled waiting rooms, eyed by myriad horse-teethed young ladies, by deftly innocuous young men. This was not the newspaper world with which Dake was familiar. The war, with its wood pulp starvation, had brought about the combine of the last two competing dailies, and during the darkest hours the paper had been down to four half-size sheets, with the ubiquitous "shurdlu" appearing in almost every story.

Now the paper was back to a respectable bulk, photo-printed on the tan grainy paper made of weeds and grasses. Here was no muted thud and rumble of presses, no bellows for "Boy!" Here was an air of sanctimonious hush.

"He will see you now, Mr. Lorin," a slat-thin female announced.

Dake went into the inner office. The window dioramas were of wooded hills, blue mountain lakes. The publisher was a small round man with matronly shoulders and a dimpled chin.

"Sit down, Mr. Lorin," he said. He held a card between thumb and forefinger, as though it were something nasty.

"I refreshed my mind, Mr. Lorin. The morgue typed me a summary. Your name, of course, was familiar to me the moment I heard it. Let me see now. Combat correspondent. Wounded. Married while on leave in '73. Wife killed by bombing of Buffalo when the suicide task force was repulsed. Returned to job as reporter on Philadelphia *Bulletin.*

24

Did a good job of covering convention in '75 and became a political columnist. Syndicated in sixty-two papers at peak. Quite a bit of influence. Frequently under fire as a 'visionary,' a dreamer. Columns collected into two books, reasonably successful. Advocated Second U.N., until India withdrew and it collapsed. Took a sudden leave of absence a year ago. Activities during the past year unknown. Suspected to hold some ex-officio position in current administration, State Department side."

"Age thirty-two, twenty-nine teeth, scimitar-shaped scar on left buttock. Very undignified wound, you know," Lorin said.

"Eh?"

"Never mind. Has anyone told you my reason for seeing you?"

"Mr. Lorin, I am terribly afraid that the . . . ah . . . philosophy behind your political theorizing of the past would not be in accord with our . . ."

"I don't want a job. I have one exclusive I want to give to you. I want to write it and I want the best and biggest splash you can give it. I came here because you have world readership."

"An exclusive? Our people dig, Mr. Lorin. We insist on that. I seriously doubt whether there could be any new development in . . . ah . . . your field which has not already been——"

Dake interrupted bluntly, hitching his chair closer, lowering his voice. "How about this sort of an exclusive, Mr. Haggins? Darwin Branson did not retire. He was given a very delicate mission by President Enfield. I worked on it with him for a year. The idea was to act as a middleman, to ease off world tension by getting all sides to do a little horse-trading. It was to be done in secrecy, and in the strictest honesty. All sides but Irania have agreed to make honest concessions. Irania was the last one. If Branson had dealt with Irania firmly and honestly, we could have had a chance to see at least five years of peace ahead of us. But I was present when Branson blew the whole scheme sky high by trying to make a second-level deal with the Iranian representative. Irania will make a token concession, of no value. Then the others will water down their concessions, and the net result will be more world tension instead of less. I doubt whether your . . . diggers have uncovered that, Mr. Haggins. I want you to make a big splash so that the world can know how close it came to temporary nirvana. It might do some good. It might be like a nice clean wind blowing through some very dusty parliamentary sessions. Your sheet is influential. I feel that your cooperation is in the public service."

Haggins looked flustered. He got up and walked to the nearest diorama as though he were staring out a window. He had a curious habit of walking on his toes. He clasped his hands behind him, wriggling his thumbs.

"You . . . ah . . . hand us a very hot potato, Mr. Lorin."

"Any good story is likely to be, isn't it?"

"As you know, in exposing corruption, venality, we are absolutely fearless."

"So I've heard," Dake said dryly.

"However, there is one consideration here which we must examine . . . ah . . . rather closely."

"And that is?"

"The possibility that our motives might be misinterpreted, Mr. Lorin. You have stated that this was all . . . secret negotiation. I refer now, of course, to the Public Disservice Act of '75. It would not give us recourse to any court of law, or any chance to state our own case. The Board might arbitrarily consider our publication of your story a Disservice to the State. You know the answer to that. Confiscatory fines."

"I feel that it is worth the risk."

Haggins turned toward him. "Risk is in direct ratio to what you have to lose, is it not?"

"That Act itself is the result of fear. If there were less fear in the world, Mr. Haggins, that Act might be repealed."

Haggins came back to the desk. Dake could see that he had reached a decision. He was more at ease. He said, "A bit visionary, Mr. Lorin?" He smiled. "We do our best, Mr. Lorin. We feel that we improve the world, improve our environment, in many modest, but effective ways.

Now you would have us take something that I can only consider as a vast gamble. If we should win, the gain is rather questionable. Should we lose, the loss is definite. By losing we would forfeit our chance to continue to do good in our own way."

"In other words, it's a lack of courage, Mr. Haggins?"

Haggins flushed, stood up, his hand outstretched. "Good luck to you, sir. I trust you will find a publisher who will be a bit more . . . rash, shall we say." He coughed. "And naturally, I will not mention this to anyone. I would not care to be accused of a personal Disservice. I am a bit too old to work on the oil shale."

Dake looked at the pink, neatly manicured hand. After a few moments Haggins withdrew it, rubbed it nervously on the side of his trousers. Dake nodded abruptly and left the office, took the elevator up the reinforced concrete shaft to ground level. Fear was a tangible thing in the world. Fear, on the government level, the business level, the personal level. Live out your neat little life and hope for the best. Fools took chances. Men carried weapons when they walked the night streets. Dake did not. His very size protected him adequately, his size and his look of dark, compressed fury.

He ate soybean steak in a small dismal restaurant and continued his search. At *Life-Look* and at *Time-Week* the brushoff was less delicate, but just as effective.

At dusk he managed an interview in a rattletrap building in Jersey City, an interview with a vast brick-red Irishman with a whisky rasp and a smell of barbershop.

The Irishman interrupted him. "Fleng the theories, Lorin. All that prono soup is over my head. You want to reach people. I've got a circulation. So let's get down to it. How about the stash, the dinero, the rupees, the happy old dollars?"

"How do you mean?"

"I'm used to fighting. Hell, I've got the most pornographic set of comic strips this side of Capetown. They're always trying to shut me down. I got a half million press run. So I do this. I put a banner head. Paid Advertising, it says. Not the opinion of the publisher, it says. I give you inside page one, and you write it and sign it. Thirty thousand rupees it costs you. Sixty thousand bucks. Lay it on the line and you can use that page for any damn thing you want. You can use it to challenge Gondohl Lahl to a personal fistfight if you want to. You'll do a labor camp stretch if that Enfield crowd doesn't like it, and Kelly will still be here, operating at the old stand. That's the deal, and take it or leave it."

"How much down?"

"The whole thing down. They'll confiscate anything you got before they ship you out. I can't take chances."

"It's a lot of money, Kelly."

"You look like a guy with a lot of money."

"I'll have to . . . check with some friends. I'll make a decision and come in tomorrow and tell you."

"If the answer is no, don't bother to come in. I won't dicker. That's the price. It stands. What are you doing tonight? I got a couple cute little Singhalese tourists lined up, and four freebees to a new private tridi way uptown."

"No thanks. See you tomorrow."

"Not too early. I expect to have a hangover."

Dake went back to the city and bought passage to Philadelphia on one of the feeder lines maintained by Calcutta International Jetways. CIJ used all Indian personnel for their major schedules, but hired U.S. personnel for the feeder lines, entrusting to them the creaking, outmoded aircraft. Once U.S.-owned airlines had linked the entire world. But, in the exhaustion following the war, with the regimentation and labor allocations that had cut travel so severely, the airlines, starved for freight and passengers, had slid inevitably toward bankruptcy, in spite of the subsidies of an impoverished federal government. Thus, when CIJ had made a reasonable offer for all lines and franchises, the airlines had taken it gladly, the investors receiving CIJ stock in return for their holdings. CIJ service was quick, impersonal, efficient. There were only two other passengers on the sixty-seat aircraft. Dake knew that CIJ took a continual loss on the New York–Philadelphia run, but maintained the frequent schedule for the convenience of the Indian nationals who supervised their investments in both cities. He leaned back in the seat for the short run. The spattered lights of the city wheeled under one wing. The other two passengers were a pair of Madrassi businessmen. They conversed in Hindi and Dake could catch words now and then, enough to know that they were talking about the Philadelphia branch of the Bank of India.

He could never quite become accustomed to being considered by the Pak-Indians a second-class citizen. Toynbee had coldly outlined the ecology of civilizations. The great wheel had turned slowly, and the East was once again the new fountainhead of vitality. Their discrimination was subtle, but implacable. In major cities Indian clubs had been established. Americans could be taken there as guests, but were forbidden membership. There had been a fad when American women had begun to wear saris, to make imitation caste marks on their foreheads. The Pak-Indian Ambassador had called on the President. Saris disappeared from the shops. Fashion magazines hinted that caste marks were crude, even rude. Everyone was happy again. For a time it had been possible to emigrate to India, that new land of opportunity. But so many had taken advantage of it that restrictions became very tight, and it was still possible, but very very difficult to manage, involving a large cash bond. Though the war of the seventies had done much to alleviate racial tension in the States, there had still been small though influential Negro groups who had joyously welcomed the dominance of a dark-skinned race in world affairs. They had soon found, to their dismay, that the Pak-Indians were supremely conscious of being, in truth, an Aryan race, and brought to any dealings with the Negro that vast legacy of hatred from the years of tension in Fiji, culminating in the interracial wars. Of Pak-India proper, only Ceylon had any percentage mixture of Negro blood, due to the African invasions of ancient years, but Ceylon was to Pak-India much as Puerto Rico had been to the United States prior to Brazilian annexation.

Indians would treat you with courtesy, even with affability, but in any conversation with them you could detect, running like a symphonic theme through the orchestration of words, their conviction that you were a citizen of a decadent nation, one that had gone beyond its peak of influence in world affairs, one that was doomed to the inevitable status of a supplicant nation, free in name only.

We had it, he thought, and we threw it away. We ripped our iron and coal and oil out of the warm earth, used our copper and our forests and the rich topsoil, and hurled it all at our enemies, and conquered them, and were left at last with the empty ravaged land. How could it have been avoided? What could we have done that we did not do? Should we have used that great moment of momentum in 1945, well over thirty years ago, and gone on to take over the planet? Should we have dropped the sword, misered our resources, and succumbed meekly during the increasing pressures of the middle sixties? How did it come about that any step we could take was wrong, that every course open to us was but a different road to a different classification of disaster? England had been dying too—just a few scant years ahead of us in the inexorable schedule, yet we had been unable to learn from her defeats, unable to cut a new channel. It was almost, he thought, as though there was some unanswerable paradox against which every world power must inevitably run and collapse. Some cold and alien influence in the world, breaking the hearts of men.

Or perhaps it is all merely our own stupidity. Our blindnesses. Our inability to see and comprehend the obvious. Perhaps we are all like Darwin Branson. Able for a time—even for a sustained length of time—to influence our environment for good, yet always failing somehow in that last crucial moment. As Branson had failed when the blindness came over him.

He wondered what Patrice would say. He dreaded seeing her. Her love was a contradiction. She seemed capable of loving every aspect of him as a human being except his final, innermost motivation.

Unscathed Philadelphia had its standard joke about itself. When, during the war, many of the executive branches of government had to be evacuated to Philadel-

phia, and when the city itself was not bombed, the Phila-
delphians proclaimed that the enemy had been smart
enough to realize that by obliterating all the red tape, they
would be helping the U. S. instead of hurting it. The air of
immunity had carried over into the present time of fear.
There was less underground construction here than elsewhere. It was a prim, old-lady city, walking through the
mud with its skirts carefully held up, not too daringly, and
with a wise and knowing air as though that old lady, in her
almost forgotten youth, had raised a bit of forbidden hell.

Deceleration thrust him forward against the straps, and
ten minutes later he was in a wheezing, clattering taxi
headed toward Patrice's unexpectedly modest home near
Upper Darby. Patrice's father had died in '71 just one
week and two days before the passage of the hundred percent inheritance tax bill. His fortune had its beginnings
back when the original Gundar Togelson had been pirat-
ing oil land from Mellon. Each Togelson since then had
increased it until the late sixties when the capital gains tax
was revised to take seventy percent of all capital gains.
After inheritance taxes, Patrice, in addition to maximum
gifts each year her father was alive, inherited about five
and a half millions. At the present time it was nearly the
last fortune left relatively intact, inside the country. Under
the impact of the confiscatory taxes many people had
managed to emigrate with their funds to economically sun-
nier lands, just as the socialist government in England had
driven many private fortunes to Bermuda and elsewhere.

Patrice Togelson, a tall, warmly built Viking girl, had
brought to Dake a deep, earthy, physical need. Yet he
knew that in the management of her money she was like
flint, and like quicksilver. Like flint in her calculating
hardness. Like quicksilver in her ability to detect the tini-
est loopholes, slide through them. They had met after he
had taken a casual swipe at her in his column, criticizing
her for buying into an Indian land deal to take advantage
of the tax concessions Washington had given the investment of Indian capital.

Patrice had appeared in his office at the *Bulletin* the
next morning, blue eyes like ice, jaw set, hair a bright flow

of autumn barley. She had leaned both fists on his desk, breasts lifting with the deep breathing of her controlled anger.

"You, my friend, are out of your depth this time," she said.

"And you, lady, are an anachronism. You are a female pirate. You are a con artist."

"You cost me more money yesterday than you'll make in your whole life."

"Then the least I can do is buy your lunch."

They glared at each other, grinned suddenly, laughed aloud and went out together. It had been at first a good friendship, even though their personal philosophies were poles apart. For two basically aloof people, it had been a warmth of friendship that had quite astonished them. They found they laughed more often when they were together. One night, in front of the November fireplace in her small home, he had kissed her, expecting it to be casual, finding it to be shockingly hungry.

They were friends, and they became lovers without losing all of friendship. She was almost six feet tall, yet built in perfect feminine scale. They laughed about being in a world too small for them. They did not use the word "love" or the word "marriage." They were faithful to each other without perceptible effort. They were discreet in an age that jeered at discretion. For a time their physical preoccupation with each other became obsessive, but when they recognized the danger of that, recognized the weakness of it, they fought free of it into a relationship which was rather like that of two semi-alcoholics who would excuse themselves for an infrequent three-day bender.

Together they acquired a sixth sense about what subjects to avoid. They knew that they were two proud, strong, dominant people, who happened to believe in different things. There was too much artillery they could bring to bear on each other. It was enough for him to see the morning sun in the warmth of her hair, hear fond laughter in her throat, hold her through her quickened times of completion.

The inevitable blowup came when he told her why he was taking a "leave of absence." It had been an unpleasant scene. Even as they fought, neither of them retreating a step, he guessed that she too was aware of the loneliness to come, the empty aching nights.

The taxi driver examined the tip, grunting something that could have been thanks, and clattered off. Dake went up the walk, knowing that no fortress was ever as well protected as this house, this small tidy house, knowing that by breaking the infra-red beams he had become target. He stood on the porch, waiting. The door was suddenly opened by the pretty Japanese maid, who gave him a gold-toothed smile and said, as though he had visited there yesterday, "Good evening, Mr. Lorin."

"Evening. Does . . ."

"She knows you are here, sir. She will be right down. A brandy, sir? I'll bring it to you in the study."

He was amused. The study was for business transactions. The lounge-living room was for friends. He wondered if Patrice were prescient. Simpler than that, perhaps. She knew him well. She knew his inflexibility. And so she would know that this was not a personal call. He sat in one of the deep leather chairs. The maid brought the brandy, an ancient bottle, and two bell glasses on a black tray. She put them on the small table beside his chair, and left without a sound.

When he heard Patrice's distinctive step he stood up quickly and smiled at her as she came into the study. Her smile was warmer than he expected. As always, she had that remembered look of being larger than life size, more vital. She wore dark red tailored slacks, a matching halter.

"Quite a tan, Patrice," he said.

"I got back from Acapulco yesterday."

"Pleasure trip?" he asked wryly, her hands warm and firm in his.

She made a face. "A good buy. Hotel property."

"With your Indian pals?"

"Uh uh. Some Brazilian pals this time."

"Both ends against the middle, Patrice?"

"Of course. How else does a girl get along?" She in-

spected him, her head tilted to one side. "You look gaun-
ter, darling. Hollow-eyed. I bet your ribs show."

"The strain of being a do-gooder."

"Aren't we being just a little bit too nasty nice to each
other?" She held her hand up, thumb and forefinger an
inch apart. "Just that much brandy, please. Would I look
too severe if I sat at the desk?"

"Not if it's where your checkbook is."

She bit her lip. "This could be interesting, couldn't it?"
She seated herself behind the desk. He took her the
brandy, went back to the deep chair.

She sipped, watching him over the rim. She set the glass
down and said, "I have a feeling we're going to spar, and it
might be nasty, and before we spoil each other's disposi-
tions, I want to say something. I've had a year to plan just
exactly how I should say it. Just this, Dake. I've missed
you. Quite horribly. I wanted, and tried, to buy you and
put you in stock. It didn't work. I've been going around
rationalizing it, telling myself that if you *could* be pur-
chased, I wouldn't want you. But I'm not that way. I wish
you *could* be. I wish you had sense enough to be. Life has
plenty of meaning without you. It had more when you
were around. I miss that increment. I'm a selfish, hard-
fisted, dominating woman, and if there's any way I can acquire you permanently, I'm going to do it."

"Okay, Patrice. Equal candor. I've missed you. I've
wished that either you or I could bend a little without
breaking. But I know that's like wishing for the moon. We
were fine until we got into a scrap about pretty basic
things. Things like selfishness, like human dignity."

"My world, Dake, is a pig pen. The smartest greediest
pig gets the most corn."

"My world is a place where there's hope."

"But we both seem to be living in my world, don't we?
Now tell me why you look haunted, and miserable,
and . . . sick at heart, Dake."

He told her. She had the knack of listening with an ab-
solute stillness, of applying her intense awareness to the
problem at hand. He told her all of it, up to and including
Kelly.

"And so you came to me."

"Asking for sixty thousand dollars. Maybe you can write it off as a charity."

"I don't believe in what you're trying to do."

"I don't expect you to. I'm begging."

"For old time's sake. Isn't that the tritest phrase in the world?" She opened a drawer, selected a checkbook, scrawled a check, tore it out. She sat, her chin balanced on her fist, waving the check slowly back and forth.

"I don't make gifts, Dake. I make deals."

"I had a hunch it wasn't going to be that simple."

"You can have this check. Once that stuff hits the streets, you're going to think a building fell on you. It is going to cost me half as much again to argue the Board into letting you run around loose. Then I'll give you thirty days' wait for the impact of what you write. If nothing happens, and I am certain nothing will, you will be the one to bend a little. You will try to accept the world on its own terms. And accept me along with it, Dake."

"Then it is a purchase, after all?"

"How much pride do you leave a lady?"

"How much pride do you leave me?" he asked harshly. "Okay. Accept the fact that I'm a monomaniac. If what I want to do fails, I'll try something else."

"Little boy with a tin bugle, waking up all the forces of decency in the world. Look, people! The cow's in the meadow, the sheep's in the corn!"

"I don't know how to say this. A man does . . . what he has to do."

"And if it's an obsession? If it's something with its roots imbedded in a childhood catastrophe? Should he continue to destroy himself? Or try to effect a cure?"

"That's almost what Branson said to me."

"You told me very emphatically that he was a god walking the earth. It looks as if he remained a god to you until he questioned your . . . sanity. And then he became a monster. Personally I like his angle of snuggling up to Ir- ania. India has been moving too fast. It balances things off a bit."

"And gives us more tension, a bigger load of fear."

"Gives mankind as a whole more fear. I'm an individual. I take my own pride in being able to take care of myself."

"Anarchy?"

"Why not? That is, if you are faster and have bigger teeth than your neighbor?"

"We can't talk at all. We never could. We never will."

Her face softened. "Oh, Dake. We *did* talk. Lots."

He sighed. "I know. Sometimes it seems as if we're . . . such a damn miserable waste of each other."

She put the check on the corner of the desk within his reach. "It's on a rupee account in a branch of the Bank of India. Need it certified?"

"No. I can cash it. No deal then? No bargain?"

She looked down at her folded hands. A strand of the soft hair swung forward, shining gold in the lamplight. "No deal, Dake. I guess it's for . . . old time's sake."

He put the check in his wallet. "Thanks, Patrice. I thought you'd be . . . a lot tougher."

She lifted her head. "I was going to be."

"Anyway, I appreciate it."

She stood up quickly, came to him, sat on the arm of the deep leather chair, leaned against him, her arm around his shoulders.

Her smile was crooked, and looked as though it hurt a bit. "I'm like your Darwin Branson," she whispered.

He looked up at her. "What do you mean?" She turned away, oddly shy.

"I'm practical. I, too, am willing to settle for . . . half a loaf."

He took her shoulders, turned her, pulled her back into his lap. Her hair had a clean spicy scent. Her lips were on holiday, from the long year apart. She kissed him with her eyes wide, blue, and terribly near in the lamplight.

CHAPTER FOUR

Kelly licked his thumb again, winked at Dake, and con-
tinued to count. "Twenty-seven, twenty-eight, twenty-nine,
thirty. Thirty thousand happy rupees. The page is yours.
Got it with you?"

"I want to borrow an office and a typewriter, Kelly. I'll
work the rest of the day and have it for you sometime tomorrow afternoon."

"It will be in Thursday's edition, then."

"I want a proof drawn on it, and a chance to check it
before you lock it up."

"At the moment you are my favorite man in all the
world. Anything you say."

"And I want a receipt, Kelly."

The man scrubbed his red chin with a big knuckle. "My
boy, you bring up a fascinating point. Indeed you do. Now
we're both men of the world. How would it be if I give you
a receipt for fifteen thousand? It would ease my tax picture considerable."

"Thirty thousand."

"Let's split the difference. I'll give you back . . . say,
two thousand, and a receipt for twenty. We both gain that
way."

"Suit yourself," Dake said wearily. "Just show me
where I can work."

"I knew you were a sensible man when I laid eyes on
you. Let me see. I can't give you Carter's place. The mu-
rals would keep your mind off your work. Come on. I
know where I can put you."

The office was small, and it hadn't been dusted in a long
time. The typewriter looked adequate. Dake tried it, using

his gunfire four-finger technique. Kelly walked out, whistling. Dake shucked his coat, tossed it on the couch. He poked his hat back onto the back of his head, laid his cigarettes beside the machine, and pondered a lead. He tried a few and tore them up. Finally he found one he was satisfied with:

"This week humanity booted the ball again. It was an infield error. The shadows stretch long across the diamond. The long game is drawing to a close. Death is on the mount. He threw one that President Enfield got a piece of. Enfield's hit put Darwin Branson on third. He had a chance to come home. He ran nicely most of the way to the plate, and then faltered. They put the tag on him. 'Yerrout!' yelled the celestial umpire.

"Now we're waiting for another decision. We're waiting to find out whether that was the third and last out, retiring the side. We stand in the long shadows, in the hopelessness of an emptying park, waiting to find out if our long game is over. To find out if, maybe, it is being called on account of darkness."

He looked at the lines. He had a sense of destiny in him. Once in every age, man and moment meet. And the man brings to that moment some ability that sets the world afire, that brings it lurching back from that last brink of destruction. The typewriter clattered in the dusty office. He worked on at white heat, working with the sure and certain knowledge that what he was writing would lift up the hearts and hopes of men everywhere. The year of leave seemed to have heightened his facility. There was no rustiness, no groping for words, or for effect. He had it, and he was using it with the pride and assurance of a man at the peak of his abilities.

He ripped a sheet out, rolled a fresh one into the machine. He hit the tab set and . . . came to a shocked standstill on the shoulder of a dusty country road. He could see the countryside clearly, hear the faraway bawling of cattle. And shimmering through it, directly in front of him, he could see the keyboard of the typewriter. It was as though he co-existed in two realities, one superimposed over the other. Standing in one, sitting in the other, visions overlapping. He managed to stand up blindly and move away from the typewriter. The countryside faded and was gone.

He stood at the window of the small office for a time. The experience had made him feel faint and dizzy. He grunted with disgust. This would be a hell of a time to have the strain of the past year pile up on him and destroy his ability to work. This was, perhaps, the ultimate gamble. Lay it on the line for them. Get it all down. Dates, names, people, the delicate machinery of deals and counterdeals. Show all the men of good will how close they had come to the political and economic equivalent of the Kingdom of Heaven. Raise the old war cry of "throw the bastards out!"—but this time on a global scale. Pray that copies of the article would be pirated, smuggled through the fine mesh nets of censorship. Patrice, with her "me for me" philosophy could never understand how a man could stake his life on one turn of the card, if he believed in the card. A man could have a sense of destiny —believe in his heart that he could manufacture a pivot-point for the world to turn on. Let us have no more double vision. No time to go mad.

He went back and sat down at the typewriter again, reread his lead, and found it good. He raised his hands a bit above the keys and stopped, shut his eyes hard. Each key had turned into a tiny reproduction of Patrice's face. With his eyes still shut he put his fingers on the keys, felt the softness of tiny faces under the pads of his fingers. He opened his eyes and looked at the paper in the machine. He began to type and stopped, as horror welled up to the point of nausea. His fingers were bloodied and the little faces were smashed, and he had heard the tiny cries, the rending of tissue. Sweating, he wiped his hands on his thighs as he stood up, knocking the chair over.

He stood with his back to the machine and tightened his muscles until his shoulders ached. He looked cautiously at his fingertips. The blood was gone. Hallucination, then. A minor madness. He thought it out objectively. Self-preservation, probably. Trying to save the organism from disaster. A glandular revolt against dissolution. He looked cautiously over his shoulder. The typewriter was sane, normal, familiar.

He sat down and began to type. His thoughts were fluent. His fingers could hardly keep up. He tore the second sheet out of the machine and read it.

"And so it is a baseball game and game and never the over of the now and the then and given. Tender and mathew and meatloaf the underside twisteth of the die and the perish now. All ye who enter can frenzied the window savior . . ."

The whole page was like that. Gibberish. Insanity. The stream of consciousness of an idiot who remembers words but has lost their meaning.

He tried again, writing more slowly. It was no good. He found a pencil in the table drawer. He took one of the copy sheets and tried to write. The pencil became too hot to hold. He examined blisters on his hand which faded even as he looked at them. The paper curled into flame, and he slapped it out. A moment later it was unscorched. He could no longer repress a primitive panic. He ran from the office and down the corridor, heart pumping, hands sweaty.

He did not quiet down until he was on the street. And suddenly he felt like an utter damn fool. Take a break and then go back and get it written. He walked to a small restaurant and sat at the counter and ordered coffee. The waitress was gray and surly with a prono hangover. A tiny radio yipped like a terrier. He listened with half his mind.

". . . and late last night Darwin Branson, retired statesman and political philosopher was committed to Bronx Psychiatric Hos——" The waitress had flipped the dial as she walked by.

"Would you mind getting that station back, miss?"

"Yes, I'd mind. He already gave all the news."

She stood braced, ready to blow up completely if he insisted. You couldn't argue with a prono hangover. He paid for his coffee, left the cup untouched and spent ten minutes on the corner before he could find a cab willing to take the long trip.

He reached the hospital at noon. He was suspected of being a reporter and the desk tried to bar him. He produced the confidential credentials Darwin had given him. The desk reluctantly put him in contact with the resident doctor assigned to the case.

The doctor was young, unimaginative, and delighted with the case.

"Lorin you said? Worked for him, eh? Well, I suppose you can take a look. We've been checking him most of the morning. Come on."

They had Branson in a private room. A nurse was in attendance. She stood up as they came in. "Respiration is ten now, Doctor. Heart forty-four. Temperature eight-six point six."

"Damndest thing I ever saw," the doctor said in a pleased tone. "Cops brought him in last night. Found him sitting in the middle of the sidewalk. Thought it was a pronie first. We checked him. He was apparently conscious. But no reaction to anything. Couldn't make the pupil contract. Couldn't find a single damn reflex."

Dake stared at the silent waxy face on the pillow.

The doctor said, holding out a clipboard, "Just take a look at this chart. This is one that's going to be written up. Pulse, respiration, temperature—every one heading down in a line so straight it could have been drawn by a ruler. This man is just like a machine running down."

"Heart forty-two, Doctor," the nurse said softly, releasing the slack wrist.

"Tried every stimulant in the books, Mr. Lorin. No dice."

"What's your prognosis?"

"He just doesn't react to anything. Thought of encephaloma at first. Doesn't check out. It looks like he's just going to keep slowing down until he . . . stops. And there's no key in the back to wind him up. Damn unprofessional opinion, I guess, but that's the best I can do. Everybody in the place has seen him and suggested things. None of them work."

"Do you mind if I stay with him?"

"How about family? We've been unable to locate any."

"There isn't any."

"You can stay around if you want. I'll send an orderly in with another chair. From the way it looks, I don't think you'll have a long wait."

"You've never seen anything like it before, or heard of it?"

The young doctor frowned. "I've never seen one before. But I've heard rumors of others. Usually important people, come to think of it. They just seem to get . . . tired."

The doctor went out. An orderly brought another chair. Dake sat on the other side of the high bed from the nurse. He was on Darwin Branson's left side. He looked at the slack hand resting on the white sheet. Time now to forget the quarrel, and remember the better things—the good talks, the flexibility and dexterity of that wise brain.

"In my gullible years, Dake, back when I used to believe in statistics, I made a personal survey of the quality of major decisions and charted them. Of course, on the quality angle, I was being a Monday morning quarterback. I came up with a neat graph which alarmed me. Men of influence all over the world, men in high places, make wise decisions and the world improves. Then, all at once, their quality of judgment becomes impaired and the world suffers for it. They move in a vast confused flock, like sack-suited lemmings. Horrors, I was face to face with a cycle. Sun spots, addling the brains of men. Some alien virus in the air. Or God, perhaps, assuring his children of their suffering on earth."

"Did you find an answer?"

"Only in myself, where perhaps each man must find his answers. I resolved to so codify my beliefs that should I ever find myself tempted to betray my own philosophy, I would merely have to refer to my mental outline and make the decision which I would have made were I not subject to the cycle. I decided to risk Emerson's indictment of small minds."

And yet, thought Dake, you turned your back on your own beliefs only yesterday. You destroyed the labor of a full year. Horrid timing. You became ill a day too late, Darwin.

No more of those long good talks, no more of the knowledge of working for the greatest good of mankind.

"Dake, we seem to supply ourselves with destructive dreams. Chief among these is the Space Dream. It goes like this: We have made such a mess of our world that it is of no use to attempt to bring order out of our chaos. So save our best efforts for the next green world. Tomorrow the moon, next week the planets, next year the galaxy. We'll spread through the heavens, and our seed will be the bronzed, steel-eyed pioneers, and their fertile women, making green wonderlands for us in the sky. That dream, Dake, eases the conscience of those who are doing less than their best. Thus it saps our energies. 'This is man's world. We must live here. We will never reach the stars.' I would like to see every man believe that. And then if, in a thousand years, we break free, it will be pure profit— and we will have something besides hate and conflict to take along with us on the gleaming ships."

Dake thought how incredible it was that Darwin Branson should, on the last day of his life, make his first venture into opportunism.

He looked at the left hand, and then looked more closely, his breath catching in his throat. He remembered the scene just before he had left to meet Smith. Branson, being left-handed, had been trying awkwardly to snip off a hangnail on the middle finger of his left hand. Dake had volunteered help, which was gratefully received. The nail had been split a bit, and so he had pared it down carefully. That was the day before yesterday. Yet right now the nail was fully as long as the others. It could not possibly grow that fast. Dake knew he had not imagined the incident. It *had* been the left hand. He reached out and took the cool slack hand.

"Please don't touch the patient," the nurse said sharply.

He released the hand, stood up and bent over to stare more closely. He looked at the slack face, comatose, dying.

"What's the matter?" the nurse demanded.

Dake glanced at her. He knew at once how far he'd get if he tried to tell her this was not Darwin Branson. They'd have him in the next room down the hall. He sat down slowly, hoping that his emotions did not show on his face.

"Dake, I believe a fiddle-playing gentleman once commented that after you have ruled out all the impossibilities, that which remains is the solution. By the same token, if after all of the impossibilities have been ruled out, you have nothing left, then you have made a mistake in classification. You have overlooked a possibility by labeling it impossible. Like a man with a pocket lighter captured by aborigines. The wise man of the tribe says that it is impossible that there is lightning captured in that silver box. He says it is impossible that there is a tiny man in there, rubbing sticks together. He says it is impossible that fire can be made by any other than those two methods. So he falls down and worships, because he finds himself in the presence of the impossible. It was his third supposition that needed reclassification."

"Darwin, how about wrongly classifying the impossible as possible?"

"Men have tried to trisect the angle because that is an impossibility that *looks* possible. Conversely, man has never tried teleportation seriously. How do we know that may not merely be a possibility which happens to *seem* impossible, and would yield to sustained attack?"

"Pulse thirty-eight," the nurse said softly.

Dake looked at the yellow-gray face. "God help me to think this out as you would have, Darwin," he said to himself.

He had classified as "possible" Branson's sellout. But, knowing the man, it could more correctly be classified as impossible. Branson had been the man who said good-bye to him when he went to collect Smith. So the man to whom he brought Smith back was not Branson. And, if the charts were right, not even human. A doll. A toy. A clever thing wound up and set in motion at a critical juncture in history for the purpose of substituting—or more correctly, sustaining—chaos in the place of possible peace and order.

Next step: Was any world power capable of creating this man-thing?

No. Reasoning: If so, the technique would have been used for greater selfish gain, and were this the first trial attempt it would have been highly unlikely that Branson would be selected.

If the pseudo-physiology of this man-thing is beyond human abilities, then the only place of origin is extra-terrestrial.

But, to assume that means also to assume that there is some valid reason for the maintenance of world disorder. He caught the error in his own logic. He was trying to judge the validity of extra-terrestrial motivations on a human basis. He could almost imagine his skull swelling with the pressure of new concepts, new modes of thought.

Okay then. Assume that interference isn't in the form of a mile-high spaceship that sits down in the front yard. Assume it is something that comes delicately, insidiously. Unnoticed. What about duration? New, or has it been always with us?

He had an answer to that which was more instinctive than logical. More Fortian than objective. Because it solved, with one swift answer, the great dismal riddle of how man—basically a creature capable of love—had been unable to live in peace in his world.

Dake could hear the soft, even voice. "Evil is not within man, Dake. Evil is man's response to outward things—to hunger, disease, pain, fear, envy, hate. Maybe it is man's answer to insecurity. Take the common denominators that are not evil. Songbirds, flowers, mother-hood. All times, all nations, all men have held them in esteem. We seem to have lost our way. Yet I cannot believe that we have turned our back on God, Buddha, Mohammed, Vishnu. Rather we have been denied them in some curious way."

The answer to the riddle of the world—lying here on this hospital bed. If it could only be proven. Prove it and then you could cry to the skies, "We have been led! We have been tortured and twisted and set against each other! We have been a culture dish into which some agency has continually dropped acid—not enough to sterilize, but just enough to make us writhe."

How would you go about it. Autopsy? He looked at the grain of the skin, the ridged nails, the gray beard stubble. Clever, clever. They could cut the body and never find a soul. But, then, they had never found one and so could not recognize the absence.

As he became more certain, he slowly became aware of his great and dangerous knowledge. Any agency powerful enough and clever enough to effect this substitution would have a quick answer ready for any human who became suspicious, who tried to broadcast his knowledge.

Where was the real Darwin Branson?

"Pulse thirty-two," the nurse said.

The young doctor entered the room again, checked the chart, talked softly with the nurse. He thumbed an eyelid back, focused a light on the pupil. Another nurse brought in a tray. The doctor pulled the sheet back, swabbed a place over the heart, injected a needle deeply, pushed the plunger, emptying the hypodermic. He took the limp wrist and counted the pulse.

"Can't kick it up one beat a minute," he said, his voice too loud for the room.

Dake barely heard him. He sat, slowly compounding his own dilemma. There was an alternative he had overlooked. The reactions in the office Kelly had loaned him had been irrational. A sign of collapse. This whole new and startling train of thought could be another sign of collapse. No hangnail. No substitution. No extra-terrestrials.

Before you could even think of proving something to the world, you had first to prove it to yourself. Either the aberrations in the office were evidences of "interference," as was the substitution, or both factors were indicative of imminent mental collapse—a collapse due to strain, overwork, tension.

He massaged the back of his neck. Funny feeling of tension there. Had it for a week. Almost a feeling of being watched. It would come and go. A feeling of a great eye focused on you. A big lens, and you were a bug on a slide.

Either one of two things happened at five minutes past three. Either Darwin Branson died, or the man-thing ran down and stopped, its function finished. Dake left the hospital. The death watch of reporters in the main lounge converged on him. He shouldered his way through, savage and silent. They cursed him as he left. He had no heart to go back to Kelly's place. The significance of the article he had wanted to write had dwindled. Either there was a vastly bigger article—or no article at all. He thought vaguely of trying to get back the thirty thousand and decided there would be time enough the next day. He walked for blocks and caught a bus over to the island. A girl with brown hair and curiously pale gray eyes took the seat beside him.

CHAPTER FIVE

The girl with the brown hair and the pale and luminous gray eyes had watched the tall figure of Dake Lorin as he boarded the bus. She stood on the corner as the bus lumbered down the block. She fished in her blouse pocket for a cigarette, drew it out of the pack between two fingers, and hung it in the corner of her mouth, lit it with a casual, vulgar snap of the cheap lighter. Smoke drifted up along the smooth brown cheek. She stood there in her cheap tight yellow dress. Chippy on the make. As good a cover as Miguel Larner had been able to devise for her.

And he had been thorough, in his remote, time-tested way, making her open her innermost screens for the hypno-fix of the cover story. You're Karen Voss. You're twenty-four.

Miguel had taped the fix from the fading brain of the actual Karen Voss. Thorough Miguel. A year back he had taken a job as a night orderly in a big hospital, smuggled the recorder in, and taken tapes off the ones on the way out of life. Better, he claimed, than inventing the cover. And it was better. It steamed the facts indelibly onto your brain patterns. No problem of learning how to stand, talk, walk or spit. And it gave Miguel a library of cover stories to apply when needed. Miguel's efficiency kept the staff down. And it overburdened the existing personnel, she thought bitterly.

She gave a drifter the cold eye, and wrinkled her nose at the reek of prono that followed him down the street. Observation first. She looked along the street slowly and found only three probables. Chances were they'd used only one Stage Two agent on this. And if the hospital was

48

hot to get at the autopsy, he'd be jackrabbit busy making the technicians see brain convolutions where there were none. Lorin would be out from under until they picked him up again.

Observation first, and then, with screens drawn tight, a quick probe at the possibles. She tried the old lady first, the dawdling window-shopper. The probe sank deep, with none of that almost metallic ping of probe against agent screen. The old lady winced and rubbed her temple. Same with the taxi driver fiddling with the motor. That was a soft mind. Babyfood mush. She hit it almost too hard. The man dropped the wrench with a clang and his knees sagged. He straightened up slowly and rubbed his eyes. She hit the third one, the man leafing through the magazine on the far corner. A good firm mind, that one. But no ping. No screens. The impact gave him a quick frown. The man took off his glasses and held them up to the light, put them back on again.

Karen Voss didn't like the next step. This was the moment when they could punish you, knock you frothing and epileptic to the sidewalk, crunching your own bones with the muscle spasms that were the penalty for carelessness.

She lifted the outer screen, with all the caution of a kid peeking under a circus tent. With it up, you had a receptivity, but not enough. You had to get all four up, one after the other, and stand there naked. The time lag in receptivity of the potential gave them time to hit you with a full broadside.

One . . . two . . . three . . . four. All up. Naked in the daylight. Naked brain-stuff itching at the thought of the plunge. She attuned herself slowly up through the bands. She began receiving in the middle range. As she suspected, a Stage Two. But distant. A good hundred yards away. And only one. She brought him into closer focus, yet remaining too remote for detection. No need. He had his hands full. She could tell by the rhythm that he was producing illusion for three, or possibly four earthlings. Get any more on the scene and he might yelp for help, and as the help might come in the form of a Stage Three, Karen decided she'd better move.

Fourthreetwoone. Clack. All back and down and tight
and trim. All armor in place. Now the bus. Three blocks
away. Four. She dropped her cigarette, stamped daintily
on it, and walked with chippy hip-switch to the corner,
bland-eyed and arrogant. She wore the Pack B on the inside of her wide stiff belt. It was handiest there. She could
casually hook one thumb inside the belt and work the
three tiny knurled wheels. Same Senarian principle as the
space cubes and the parent web, limited by the speed of
thought. But even the Senarians couldn't give you anything but a primer version. Any more than they could
repair anything beyond the simplest circuits in that huge sat-
ellite brain that circled their old home planet, and was
such a shrine to the heart planets. And that brain, built by
the Senarians' remotest ancestors had given them the parent web and the Pack B too many thousand years ago to
count.

She could remember the manual you got at Training T
when they broke you in on the Pack B. "The Pack B must
be considered as a device to focus and concentrate the
power of thought. Practice in visualization is highly important in utilization of Pack B. The student will carefully examine each detail of a selected portion of the game field.
The student will then walk one hundred paces from that
spot. The student will imagine himself standing on that selected spot with all the power of concentration and visualization. The first wheel, marked (1) in the illustration, reduces the effective value of the mass of the student to a
minus power. The second wheel, marked (2), must be set
for the desired range. Set the second wheel first. Visualize.
Turn the first wheel one-half revolution clockwise. Turn
the third wheel, marked (3), one click. If visualization is
strong enough the third, or selector wheel, will reinstate
effective mass at the point of visualization. After practice
this can become an almost instantaneous factor. The
effective range is ten thousand yards. This same principle
activates the parent web and the space cubes, though in
that instance, the visualization, being generated by the
parent web, is of such a high order, and the power source
is so great, that there are no effective limits to the range.

The speed of thought is the final barrier. Beyond that any further acceleration would be contra-temporal."

But of course one could not go about among the earthlings appearing and disappearing. It would upset them. Miguel became furious if you didn't use the utmost caution. Get away from prying eyes when you make the jump. You have two seconds of relative invisibility at the new location. So use those two seconds to make certain you are not observed, and if there's a chance, click it again to select the departure point and try again.

She moved into a sheltering doorway, made certain no one could see her, and then visualized herself standing on a corner watching the bus lumbering toward her a half block away. She brought into sharp focus the details of the bus.

Two, one, three. A twisty little wrench in the head, and there's the bus, heading for you. She looked around quickly. One man in range. To him she would be the faintest silvery shimmer. She stepped behind a post, felt the quick flooding weight. She patted her brown hair, favored the man with an insolent look of appraisal. Stuffy Miguel would have frowned at that post routine. The man looked faintly startled at not having noticed her before, probably.

She pulled herself up onto the bus, dropped her fare in the box and went back, pleased to see that Lorin was sitting by himself. She eased down beside him with a pleased little sigh. Poor bewildered earthling. A good somber strength in that face. Good level mouth on him. Suddenly she remembered a very ordinary trick that she had almost overlooked. She probed quickly and lightly, felt no screen. She sighed again.

Illusions for the big man. It would take illusions to get him back to Miguel without risk of interception. Too bad direct control was so readily detectable, so obvious that anyone could catch it with just the first screen down, and catch it a mile away or more.

Trouble with illusions, they made the earthlings crack so easily. And Miguel wanted him intact. The bus speakers droned their inevitable commercials. And this lad had already had a liberal dosage of illusion.

She cast about for a reasonable idea, something that wouldn't disrupt the other passengers. She saw a vast fat man pull himself aboard, come down the aisle sweating and puffing. The sudden hard jolt against her outermost screen shocked her. The brain made its lightning calculation of probability. She pulled all screens tight, probed the fat man. In the same split second as the hard expected "ping" occurred, she slid the stud on the catch of her handbag—a fraction of a second too late. He had blanketed her, and she retaliated quickly. Deadlock. Neither of them could yell for help now. She turned casually. He had taken the seat behind them. She looked into his bland eyes.

This time, she realized with sinking heart, they had miscalculated badly. Miguel Larner, in spite of the Branson fiasco, had thought he could retrieve it with the assignment of two Stage Two agents. So far she could count five that Shard had assigned.

The fat man tried a probe again. Apparently he thought she was a Stage One, who could be broken down. It reduced her respect for him, but that respect returned immediately as she realized he had used it as a feint, that he was busy on an illusion. A very respectable illusion. A uniformed policeman angrily waving the bus into a side street. It was almost real enough to deceive her. She thought quickly. Block the side street with something.

A blow crashed against the back of her head. As she fell forward off the seat, she cursed her own stupidity in not thinking of a definite physical attack, the most elementary move, and therefore one of the cleverest. Though consciousness slipped a bit, she held the screens tight, recovered. Lorin was helping her up.

"That fat guy hit me in the back of the head, mister!"

Lorin turned. "What's the idea, friend?"

This time Karen Voss was ready with the illusion. The fat fist struck Dake Lorin in the face so quickly that Karen guessed Dake had no chance to notice that the fat man's arms had stayed at his sides. She was pleased to note that Lorin had beautiful reflexes. The fat man's head snapped back and he crumpled in the seat. She probed deeply and viciously, realizing with satisfaction that Shard would be minus one Stage Two agent until probe wounds healed, in six months. She had broken through the first two screens.

She saw a chance to simplify things. Illusion made the fat man's head flop over at a crazy angle. This could be done with artistry. She gave the passengers a loud male voice. "Hey, you killed him!"

She took the stunned Lorin by the arm. "Come on, let's get off this thing. There's going to be trouble."

She yanked the cord and pushed at Lorin, followed him to the front of the bus. He got off blindly. She took his wrist. "Come on." People yelled at them. No one pursued. They would quiet down when they saw the fat man was all right.

Karen hurried down the block with him and around a corner. She stopped and leaned against the side of a scabrous building, dipped again into her blouse pocket to bring out a cigarette and hang it on her lower lip. Lorin lit the cigarette for her with a hand that trembled. She could sense his emotions. Distaste for her, annoyance with the situation, a vague shame that he had run. She knew that he was a troubled man, as who wouldn't be with the illusions Shard's agent had provided for him to block the newspaper article. Yet she was slightly uneasy. She had studied Branson and Lorin. She knew them well. And now Lorin seemed a bit *too* upset. She wished she dared take him under full control. He might be hard to handle.

"I cert'ny want to thank you, mister."

"That's all right. I hope I didn't get us in trouble, miss."

"Karen. Karen Voss. I bet I know you. I bet you're Dake Lorin. I used to see your picture next to your column all the time."

He looked mildly pleased. "Don't tell me you used to read it."

"Sure. Maybe you wouldn't think so. I go for that stuff. Politics, economics, international relations. I got a friend. He's got money. Lots of money. He was saying just the other day he'd like to see you back in business. He says you used to make a lot of sense. Maybe he'd back you— buy space in a paper or something."

"The Public Disservice Act keeps anyone from saying anything very critical, Miss Voss. I don't think your friend would want to join me on a shale pile."

She snorted. "Nobody touches him. Not twice anyway. I guess you heard of him. Miguel Larner."

"The racketeer? Certainly I've heard of him. He's got his hands in every filthy . . ."

"Don't go Christer, Mr. Lorin. Mig has got . . . well, two sides to his nature. He might be a lot of help to you." She was secretly amused at her words. "He's a good friend of mine. Want to see him?"

"I don't think so."

"Maybe you're in some kind of trouble. He likes helping people. You wouldn't think so, would you? But he does."

"I don't think there's anything he can do for me."

"You in a rush? You got an appointment or something? It isn't far."

She could sense his indecision. She urged him gently. At last he agreed reluctantly. She broke the connection by sliding the stud on the catch of her bag. Miguel would have heard Lorin agree. He'd be ready. She walked beside the tall man, alert for any form of interception. She hailed a cab, settled back in the seat beside Lorin, giving him a mechanical sultry smile, crossing her round brown legs.

By the time they reached 215th Street he said, accusingly, "Not far?"

"Just a couple more blocks, honey."

The cab let them out. Lorin paid the fare. She saw his quick curious glance at the sleek above-ground lobby. As they passed through the doorway Karen felt the barrier break, fold shut again behind them. She gave the traditional sigh of relief that came up from the stubbed toes of her shabby pumps. Nothing could touch her in here. Nothing could reach into the warm security of the egg-shaped barrier. The pointed end of the egg was above-ground, making a small dome over the entrance. The rest of the egg encircled all of the levels below-ground. Here Miguel Larner, Stage Three, presided over the agent teams, routed the field operations, maintained the communications network. Usually, the moment she was inside, she could erase the Karen Voss hypno-fix temporarily and revert to her own identity. But with Lorin in tow she had to keep her makeup on.

The Stage One at the desk had been alerted.

"We want to go down and see Mr. Larner, Johnny." *How did I do?*

"I guess you can go right on down, Miss Voss." *Nice going, lady.*

"Thanks, Johnny." *And scratch one Stage Two.*

"You're welcome, Miss Voss." *Don't get too many credits. We'll miss having you around.*

She led the way back to the elevator. As it slid silently down the shaft she gratefully let the rest of the screens slip. She had released the first one to permit communication with the Stage One at the desk. She felt warmly proud of herself, knowing that she had come out of this with a credit. *One step closer to the heart worlds, my girl. One step closer to Training T to become a Stage Three, and then one more tour and you're out of it, and you can go to work. Next time, by God, they'll have to do better than this chippy cover. The fix went a little too deep. You had to watch your reflexes.*

"Have you known Larner long?"

"A pretty long time. Here we are." The door slid back and they walked directly from the elevator into the main room of Larner's suite. It was a garish room, furnished with the best that Bombay supply houses could offer. One whole wall was a vast and intricate diorama, portraying a walled garden with a pool. Miguel spent a lot of his time by the pool, and the perspective was so cleverly done that it gave the impression of being a vast open space, rather than a twenty by twenty cube cut into bedrock. Miguel kept the controls set in such a way that the diorama changed through each hour of the twenty-four, from cloudless days to full-moon nights.

Miguel was sitting out by the pool in the four o'clock sunlight, a chunky sun-browned man with very little forehead and eyes like oiled anthracite. He wore lemon-yellow bathing trunks, and had a glass in his hand.

He waved casually. "How's it going, Karen? Come on out. Who's your friend?"

They went out by the pool. "Don't you recognize him, Mig? It's Dake Lorin." *Is this going to be one or two credits? I broke down a Stage Two.*

Miguel reached up with a languid hand. "Nice to know you, Mr. Lorin." *I suppose you were too busy congratulating yourself to scan properly. Take another look and see why it's only one credit for not seeing the obvious.*

"I was telling Dake how you always liked his stuff, Mig." *All right, so I missed it. But when you assign two and they assign five, it keeps you busy. I see what you mean. Carelessness. Something about a fingernail.*

"I've missed your column, Mr. Lorin. Used to get a charge out of it, the way you hacked at everybody." *Yes, they should have had somebody there ready with an illusion, checking to see if Lorin accepted the doll.* "Have a drink, folks? Sit down."

They took poolside chairs. "Gee, I'd go for a collins. How about you, Dake?" *Are you getting what I'm getting, Miguel? He's balanced on the edge. It's a little beyond his credibility, and he is wondering about his own sanity.*

Miguel pushed a button. The servant appeared almost at once. He gave the orders. *So we must be very careful, girl. A little push might send him over the edge. Once we use him, maybe we can run a check and see. But I don't think he'd make it. Rigidity there. Father image. Streak of the Puritan. Somber messiah. They seldom check through. Too dependent on the nature of reality.*

"Hasn't Mig got a nice place here, Dake?" *Don't forget the quota. He might do very nicely.*

"I guess I could be classified as unemployed right now, Mr. Larner," Dake said. "I've been working for the government for a year. And today my . . . superior died. A bit suddenly. It was sort of unofficial employment, so I guess that ends it."

"Weren't you working for Branson?" Miguel asked.

"Why, yes! How did you know that?"

"I got sources. I have to keep in touch. Anything

Branson did might effect imports and exports. And anything that effects those, changes my income. You got any plans, Mr. Lorin?"

"I'm writing a newspaper article for Thursday publication."

"Hot?"

"It would have been hotter if Mr. Branson hadn't died. It will probably be classified as a Disservice to the State."

"Putting your head in the noose, eh?"

"I suppose you could call it that. It just seems . . . more important than what can happen to me. Trouble, though, is that it's critical of Darwin Branson. He's the man who died today."

"You need a place to work?"

"Thanks, no. A man is letting me use an office."

"If it doesn't work out, I got a place here you can use. A nice setup." *Do you want to fix Kelly, girl? Now that we have him here I want him to stay.*

"This would be a nice quiet place to work, Dake," Karen said. *Let Dale do it. I've been outside too long. It made hash of my nerves, Miguel. See how restless he is getting? He wants to leave.*

"I changed my mind, Karen," Miguel said. "This is easier. I just put him under full control."

She looked quickly at Lorin, saw the automaton rigidity of his posture, the eyes in trance. *But how can you . . .*

"Aloud, please. Para-voice is an insidious habit on tour. The easiest way to keep him here is to take full control. Let him believe he went back to Kelly and Kelly changed his mind and gave him a refund of his money, and backed out. Then we'll release him up above in the lobby with the idea he has come here to take up my offer. It just seems simpler. Ready now, and I'll turn him over to you. Take him to one of the rooms upstairs and give him the complete memory pattern of seeing Kelly and coming back here at, say, nine this evening. Leave him in stasis up there and then you can rest and take him up to the lobby at nine."

Karen waited. When Miguel released Lorin she caught him deftly. There was a split second of release in which

Lorin stirred and made a faint sigh, almost a moan. Then she had him. As she went through the wide doors into the main room and toward the elevator, she looked back and saw him following her with that odd walking-on-eggs stride of the controlled. There was always a pathetic vulnerability about the controlled which touched her. It seemed particularly poignant in this case, all the tall hard strength of the man following as docile as a lamb.

She took the elevator up two levels and walked him down a corridor to an empty room. Lorin sat on the edge of the bed, turned stiffly, lifted his feet up, and lay back, eyes open and staring, arms rigid at his side.

Karen sat on the edge of the bed and quickly took him through all the mechanical actions of returning to New Jersey, talking to Kelly, listening to the man's protestations, accepting the refund, returning to the city. She took him on an aimless walk, had him eat a solitary meal, decide to take Miguel's offer, and return to the apartment. She stopped the visualization the moment he stepped through the door, through the barrier. It was the work of but five minutes to give him the entire visualization, and it took another few seconds to push consciousness even further back so that he would remain in stasis until she called to get him.

With an impulse that surprised her a bit, she bent over and kissed his unconscious lips lightly. Poor big oaf. Poor bewildered earthling, torn this way and that. Pawn in a game he'd never know. She kissed her fingertip, touched the middle of his forehead, smiled down at him, and left the room, shutting the door quietly, even though it would have made no difference at all if she had slammed it.

CHAPTER SIX

Kelly stubbornly pushed the money back across the desk.
He said, "Now take it, Mr. Lorin. I already told you. I've
reconsidered. I don't think that disclaiming the article
would give me enough immunity. They'd wonder why I
accepted it."

Dake wearily pocketed the money, stood up. "I guess
there's nothing I can do but look for someone else."

Kelly leaned back in his chair. "Now if you'd come to
me with a little better backing. Say with a note from Mig
Larner, or somebody like that . . ."

"What made you mention his name?"

"I was just using him as an example. If Mig says you
won't get in trouble, you won't. He keeps all the right
wheels greased, that lad does."

Dake left Kelly's place. It was after six. He had a long
search for a cab. Once he was back in Manhattan he got
off at New Times Square. Strange day. Darwin . . . or
what was supposed to be Darwin . . . dying like that. He
felt strange. Almost unreal. It was an odd sensation, as
though his side vision were impaired, as though he could
only see straight ahead, and everything else was a grayness, a nothingness. It was the same with sounds. He kept
hearing sharp individual sounds, but the background
noise of the city seemed to be missing. It seemed to him
as though there were some serious impairment of all his
senses. Yet, oddly, he could not seem to bring himself to
stop and check that impairment—to turn his head
quickly, to listen consciously for all the background noise.
And those people he did see, those normal characters of
the streets were subtly altered. Colors had slightly dif-

ferent values. And his instinctive and automatic appraisals seemed distorted.

He saw a lovely girl looking into a cluttered shoddy store window, examining the ersatz fabrics. He found himself looking at her with a peculiar feeling of envy and jealousy. And he was conscious of the breadth of shoulder of the men. He could not be certain, or even investigate the fact, but he had the wry idea that he was mincing along rather than walking. The world had a dreamlike aspect, and it seemed to him that, almost on an unconscious level, he was trying to tell himself that he was dreaming, yet not being able to force the thought up to the level of action.

He found a quiet restaurant where he had never been before. He ordered a sweet drink which normally he despised. And found it surprisingly good. He ordered a very light meal, and yet it seemed to satisfy him completely. The world was a bit out of focus, and yet he could not capture his wandering attention and apply his intelligence to a thorough appraisal of exactly where and why it was out of focus.

After he finished the meal he decided that the next step was definitely to return to see Miguel Larner. He decided to work it from a different angle this time. Complete the article, and then find someone willing to print it, either free or for a fee. Let the article speak for itself. Let the public learn exactly what Stephen Chu and Garva had been willing to do. Let them learn about the trade concessions Gondohl Lahl had promised. Let them learn that the enemy coalitions were, behind their brave front, pathetically eager to effect a compromise, achieve a period of stability. And show them all how the conversation with Smith had destroyed this chance.

He was surprised at how quickly time had gone. He stepped out of the cab in front of Larner's place at nine o'clock, paid the man and walked into the lobby. He walked in and stumbled on the smooth floor for no reason at all, caught himself. There had been an odd little twist, or click, and now side vision had returned, he could hear the full range of sound, colors had their former values.

That odd girl from the bus was leaning on the clerk's desk. Voss. Karen Voss. He wondered why he hadn't wasted a single thought on the fat man in the bus since leaving Larner's place that afternoon. Pretty damn callous to kill a stranger and forget it.

"Hi there, Dake," Karen said. "Just talking about you. Remember the fat man on the bus?"

"I certainly do."

"I guess it looked worse than it was. You just knocked him out. Heard that he's okay. I had Mig check on it."

"I still can't understand why he hit you. I'm damn glad to hear he's okay."

"Maybe I reminded him of somebody who picked his pocket once. And maybe I did. I've got a lousy memory. How do you like the dress?"

She whirled the full skirt. He said, "I guess I like it. Little daring, though. That style is older than you know. The women of Crete started it a long, long time ago."

"All I know is that Mig had it flown over from Madras." She took his arm. "Mig is psychic. He told me you'd be back. I'll go down with you. 'Bye, Johnny." *I'm starting to like this big lug. Did you see him blush? That's a lost art.*

"Come back, Miss Voss." *Don't get the geef over any earthling, lamb. There's no future in it.*

Poo.

On the way down in the elevator, Dake felt his cheeks grow hot again. He said, "Are you a . . . uh . . . special friend of Mr. Larner?"

She squeezed his arm. "I guess I give him a few laughs. That's all."

He was embarrassed at his own show of interest. There was something pleasingly childlike about this Karen Voss, but he knew that she was one cheap, tough, hard little article. It was in her stance, her eyes, the shape of her mouth. That opaque quality of sexual arrogance of one of those little girls who have learned too much too fast.

"Does Mr. Larner ever go out?"

"Why do you ask that?"

"I just had the strong feeling that he didn't. That maybe he wouldn't be safe on the outside."

He looked down into speculative luminous gray eyes. She was standing so close to him that he could see the little amber flecks that ringed the pupil. He decided that it was the high quality of the intelligence of those eyes which was so startlingly at odds with the chippy walk, the too-tight clothes, the insolent curve of lip.

"Not as bright as all that," she said.

He stared at her. "How did you know what I was thinking?"

For a moment she looked genuinely disconcerted. Then she threw her head back and her throat pulsed in a raw vulgar bellow of laughter. "Jesus H. Gawd," she gasped. "Now I'm getting psychic yet. Or maybe we're soulmates, sugar. Ever think of that?"

Miguel Larner was in his diorama garden, in the long sweet dusk of a midsummer evening which contrasted with the October night in the city above. Sound tracks gave to scrupulous perfection the muted night-cries of insects, the fluid silver of a distant nightingale, the garrump of a conclave of frogs in a bog on the far side of the meadow.

"Hey, Mig! He came back like you said." *And he caught me off guard in the elevator. I could swear he was sending on the para-voice band, and doing it perfectly.*

"Sit down, people. Glad you came back, Lorin. Especially if it means I can help you." *I noticed how clear he was this afternoon. A latent, perhaps.*

Dake sat down as soon as Karen was seated. "As a matter of fact, the man who was going to print the article backed out. And returned my money. That didn't seem in character. I've got it here. I thought perhaps you could ——That's damn funny! I put it right here in this pocket."

Girl, you seem to be making a habit of being careless with this one.

Karen laughed. "A demonstration, Dake. I wanted to

show you how an expert picks a pocket. I did it on the elevator." *Decent recovery, Miguel?*

Thirty thousand rupees, girl. Let's see the illusion.

Dake took the money Karen handed him. He handed it to Miguel. "Here's thirty thousand rupees, Mr. Larner. I wonder if you could use it to get me a spot where the article will get a decent readership."

If he's a latent, Miguel, wouldn't that help?

Screens raised, eh. Afraid I'll see the sudden emotional interest in this one.

Let me give him a strong primary impulse and see if he's latent receptive too.

All this will wait until we've used him as a counter-move against Shard. In another moment I might get impatient with you, girl.

Miguel took the money, shoved it casually into his shirt pocket. "Lorin, you're not hiring me with this. I'm just keeping it for you. You go ahead and write the article. I'll find a spot for it. And give you the change. Why don't you stay right here? One of my secretaries is on vacation. Complete apartment with no one in it."

"I wouldn't be in the way?"

"Not a damn bit. Give me your local address and I'll send somebody over for your stuff."

"Just a hotel room. I've been living in hotel rooms every since going with Branson."

"I'll have you checked out then."

Dake gave Miguel the name of the hotel. Miguel said, "Show him where he hangs his hat, Karen. Next floor above, Dake. End of the hall. Give Johnny a ring, Karen, and tell him Mr. Lorin is in 7 C, for an indefinite stay."

They left the diorama garden. Dusk had faded into night. Karen took him up in the elevator and down to 7 C. The door was unlocked. Karen went in first, flipping the light switches, activating the diorama. It was a moonlit seascape with a sound track of waves against the beach.

"Very luxurious," Dake said.

What?

"I said it's very luxurious." He glanced at her, wondered why she wore such a smug look, as though she had proved something to herself.

"It's got a liquor cupboard too, Dake. Build you a drink?"

"If you'd like. I think I need a drink. This has been . . . one of the craziest days of my life."

She had her back to him, sitting on her heels, looking into the liquor cabinet. *Scotch okay for you?*

"Are you a ventriloquist or something, Karen?"

She turned toward him. "Why?"

"Your voice had the funniest quality right then. It seemed to come from all corners of the room at once."

"Used to sing a little. Maybe that's it. Why has this been a crazy day, Dake?"

"I ought to talk to somebody. Just let me ramble, even if it doesn't make sense to you. That sounded pretty superior, didn't it?"

"Not too. You couldn't expect me to follow everything you could say."

She brought him a tall drink. "Kashmiri Dew. Eight years old." She perched on the arm of his chair, rather disturbingly warm against his arm. "Mind?"

"N-no. I guess what's troubling me the most is wondering if I'm losing my mind."

"Don't they say that if you're wondering about it, you aren't?"

"I don't have much faith in that. I've always been a sort of functional pragmatist."

"Don't make the words too big, Professor."

"If I could see something, feel it, touch it, smell it, hit it with my fist, then it existed. And my actions were based on thought which in turn was based on realities."

"I sort of get it, sugar."

"So today reality began to go sour on me. Typewriter keys don't bleed. A man's fingernail doesn't grow a quarter of an inch in two days. And ever since I left here this afternoon, until I got back, everything was curiously unreal. Like I was walking and talking in a dream. When I couldn't find that money in my pocket, I began to think it *was* a dream."

"What's this typewriter keys and fingernails routine?"

"Little things where my senses didn't send the right messages to my brain. As if I suddenly saw you walk across the ceiling."

"Shall I?"

"Don't look at me like that. I begin to think you can. Anyway, what has a man got to hold onto except reality?"

"Okay, sugar. I rise to ask a question. I'll name a list. Faith, hope, love, honor. Can you touch them, smell, them, hit them with your fist?"

"Those items are the result of thought regarding other concrete items which can be detected with the senses."

She turned and kissed him suddenly. Her eyes danced. "I'm beginning to get it, Professor. You could feel that, couldn't you. But if it ended up in you loving me, you would only get that from . . . from inference."

"I get the damndest feeling that you're way ahead of me. And don't do that again."

"If you don't like it, I won't. Let's continue the discussion, Professor. Let's play suppose. Like that guy Midas. Everything he touched turned to gold. Okay. According to you he should have gone nuts. But he didn't. He starved to death. What was that? Strong brain? Suppose an ordinary guy. A guy like you. His world starts to frazzle on the edges. Wouldn't he have enough pride to keep telling himself that he was okay? That something was doing it to him, on purpose?"

"Persecution complex, eh. So he's crazy anyway."

"Suppose another thing. Suppose this precious reality of yours that you like so well, suppose all that is fiction, and when you begin to see crazy things, you're seeing the real reality."

"You have a very unique mind, Karen."

"The adjective has been used on me before. But not that way, sugar."

"You should have done more with yourself. That quality of imagination is rare."

"You know, Dake, you're a little on the stuffy side. How about if I like me the way I am? How about that?"

He grinned. "My reformer instinct always crops out. Forgive me."

"You said it was funny this afternoon after you left here. How?"

"Colors looked odd. People looked odd. I had the feeling that I wasn't seeing or hearing as much as I should."

"So this style started in Crete. How veddy veddy interesting!"

He quickly averted his eyes and felt his face get hot again. She laughed at him. "It's no trick to read your mind sometimes, Lorin, man."

"Look, I don't want to be too stuffy, but . . ."

"I have the idea Patrice wouldn't care."

He frowned at her. "Dammit, that's about enough. I know I didn't mention her to you. You've got a lot of extra-sensory perception or something."

"I read the gossip columns. Sort of a cold dish, isn't she?"

"Miss Voss, you pry. Now, out! I'm going to try to do some work."

She slid off the arm of the chair, winked blandly at him. "All right, dear. Use the phone for food. They bring it down. All the office stuff is through that door. Your clothes and things ought to be over soon."

She went to the door, burlesquing her normally provocative walk. She winked again, over her shoulder, and left. He sat for a time thinking of what she said about reality. What if all the "normal" things were illusionary, and all the things that went bump in the night were fragments of reality, seen through the mist of illusion? He shrugged off the idea. Maybe a table top *is* a matrix of whirling bits of energy. Maybe all the true matter that makes up a man, once you eliminate the spaces between nucleus and perimeter electrons, *is* no bigger than the head of a pin. But you can beat on a table with your fist, and the wood hurts your hand. And you can break a man's jaw and hear the bone go.

He found that the small office was beautifully equipped, and as clean as an operating room. He worked on the article, regaining the free flow of words which he had experienced in the office borrowed from Kelly. He used the same lead, tightening it a bit, altering it to include the death of Branson.

After an hour of work he went out to phone for food. He was famished again. His clothes had been brought, neatly unpacked in the bedroom. The food was brought. He worked for another hour and then went to bed. He sat on the edge of the bed in his pajamas. He put his feet up and lay back. A funny example of *déjà vu,* he thought. As though he *had* been in this room before. Or a room very like it. With Karen. She had sat on the edge of the bed. Later she had kissed his lips. She had told him something. Something about Kelly. It was so difficult to . . .

Sleep came quickly. The dream was as crazy as the day. Myriad voices echoing inside his skull. He couldn't get them out. They were little people, trudging around in there. Pinching and prodding his brain. Nibbling at the edges with tiny rodent teeth. Yelling at each other. All talking at once. Commenting on him. Hey, look at this. And this over here! What do you know? Pinch and prod and nibble, and all the voices going like too many records playing at once. Definitely latent. And a receptive. But a fracture line here, and here. Father image. Won't do. Won't do at all. But look at this!

He woke up, sitting up, hearing his own roar of "Get out!" still lingering in the silent air-conditioned room. He was sweaty and chilled. He pulled the blanket up over him. He could hear faint music. Very odd music. He couldn't recognize the instruments. Probably some new Pak-Indian fad, he decided. Damn stupid to accept Miguel Larner's hospitality. Well, use any means if the end is good. Damn destructive philosophy, however, if you overdid it. Question. Who was using who, whom?

CHAPTER SEVEN

————*It was a fine summer morning on Manarr. The* sun beamed hot on the shallow placid seas, on the green rolling traces of the one-time mountains. The fi-birds dipped over the game fields, teetering on membranous green wings, yelping like the excited children. Picnic day. Picnic day. Everyone was coming, as everyone had always come. Hurrying from the warm pastels of the small houses that dotted the wide plains, hurrying by the food stations, the power boxes. Hooray for picnic day. The smallest ones set their tiny jump-sticks at the widest settings and did crazy clumsy leaps in the warm air, floating, sprawling, nickering. The maidens had practiced the jump-stick formations and groups of them played towering floating games of leapfrog on the way to the game fields, spreading wide their skirts, swimming through the perfect air of this day. The young men watched and bounded and set their jump-sticks narrow to do the hard quick tricks. Picnic day. Today there would be water sculpture, and sky dancing, and clowns. Day of laughter, evening of the long songs, night of mating. Time for work tomorrow. The hard work that cramped the brain and so often brought tears, under the unforgiving eye, the cold trim face of the earthling. Someone had said that today the earthling would judge the water sculpture, lead the sky dance. Few believed it.

————Ten parsecs beyond the outermost star system the great ship rested. It had been built in space. No planet crust could withstand its weight, and thus it had never felt the full tug of gravity at close range. It was the flagship

68

for a full division. On the master control cube, three dimensional diagram of a galaxy, tiny red spheres showed the placement of each ship of the division. In this hour it was a nervous ship. Quick flick of eyes. Lick of tongue tip across dry lips. Silence. The launch had arrived an hour ago. At last the bell called all officers. They hurried to central assembly, stood in formation at attention.

After five minutes the earthling arrived, with his cold and bitter eyes, the flat iron slab of a face, wearing his symbols of command. The prisoner was taken to the vast open space in the middle of the hollow square of the formation.

They said he could give you a writhing agony with a mere glance, read your most secret thoughts, turn you to a mindless thing. The officers stood like statues.

The harsh voice of the earthling filled the huge room. "Officers. Observe the prisoner. He commanded a ship. He forgot the need for endless vigilance." The prisoner stood with a face like death.

"They came once. They came out of the blackness between the galaxies. They would not communicate. They were merely a patrol. Yet it took the total strength of the galaxy to hurl them back. They will come again, in strength. We are stronger now, yet not strong enough. The prisoner grew bored with vigilance. For two thousand years there has not been one second of relaxation. Nor will there be until they return, as they inevitably will. Remove the prisoner."

He was marched away, head bowed.

The earthling said, in a quieter tone, "Defense cannot remain static. Every ship in this division is obsolete." There was a stir and murmur in the ranks of officers.

"The first ship of the new class is being assembled. It has better shields, heavier weapons, a new and more effective hyper-drive. This crew has been selected for immediate return and training. I shall transfer command headquarters to one of your sister ships. On your return with the new ship I will once again command the division from your ship. Within five years complete replacement of the ships of this division will be effected. Obsolete ships will be placed in reserve. Patrol areas will be twice as far from the galactic rim as we are now. I have recommended brief leave for each of you on his or her home planet. Dismissed."

————At Bionomic Research they had all been uneasily aware of the new earthling who had replaced gentle, easygoing The'dran. But the long days drifted by and they slowly became used to his habit of roaming through the low gray buildings. They prepared the metal tapes which listed, in minute detail, the almost infinite ecological factors of the unbalanced planets and fed them through the whispering calculators, getting the slow results that so often looked like utter nonsense. It was very slow work, but who could hasten it? Nature moved slowly. If the answer was to eliminate one certain type of shrub on such and such a planet, who was to hasten it? In perhaps fifty of the planet years in question, elimination of the shrub would have caused the extinction of a certain class of insect which in turn was the food source for a specific class of lizard which restricted the natural watershed by tunneling too indiscreetly among tree roots and stunted growth.

So they began to accept the earthling as a symbol, and nothing more.

Until one day, in a cold flat voice, and with unfriendly eyes, he called them parasites and time-wasters and fools. He revised all the old ways, formed them into research teams, assigned one field team to each research team, demanded synchronized recommendations, with a target date for putting them into effect. The old ways were gone. The slow warm days. Now it was hurry, hurry. Planets must be bionomically balanced, with resources utilized toward the setting of an optimum population level. Transportation of necessities between planets is a waste. Hurry, hurry, hurry. It should have been done yesterday, the day before yesterday. Please the earthling with your energy, or end up at Center with your technical qualification erased and your number changed to manual labor.

————On Training T, far from the power webs, far from the intricate geometric pattern of the space cubes, gleaming on the vast metallic plain, far from the black training buildings and the instruction beams, a Stage Two wept. The mind, seemingly strong, flexible, elastic, had not been able to take the Stage Three instruction. A hidden fracture line. They would not go on with it. Another attempt would result in mindlessness. He was a strong, bitter, powerful man, graduate of the Irish slums of New Orleans. With fists and teeth and grinding ambition he had fought his way up. And he wept because here, so very clearly, so very precisely, was the end of the line. Yet a young girl—linguist, dreamer, poet—had made it, knew what her assignment would eventually be.

————In Madrid, behind the egg-shaped barrier that enclosed and concealed the luxuries of the sun-bleached castle, Shard checked the agent credits, made out his requisition for personnel. Forty Ones, sixteen Twos, two Threes. No Stage Three could keep track of his own credits. He realized sourly that the filling of the requisition in total would be his only indication that he had served well in this, his third tour. He yearned to be rid of the stinking, brawling, sniveling billions, to be clear of the miasmic stench of fear and hate. Endless battle for a world. An endless stirring of the pot.

He asked that the Gypsy girl be brought in. She had a boldness he liked, a boldness stronger than her fear. He produced illusions for her, watching her mind closely, always slanting the illusions more and more closely toward the secret focus of all her fears. Knives and worms and things with claws that crawled. Nineteen, she was, yet through her man she had been leading her tribe of *gitanos* for over two years, and leading them with an iron will, leading them well.

He turned her breasts to lizard heads and her fingers to tentacles and she fainted, blood on her mouth. Yet when she revived, she spat at him and cursed him, with *flamenca* fury. She would do. One of the unbreakable ones. One of the precious bitter ones.

Shard took her down the slanting tunnel to the small
space station. He took her personally. A signal honor. He
touched the stud and the orifice slit in the gray cube
opened. He thrust her in, reached in and touched the
guide stud for Training T, stepped back. The cube shim-
mered, iridescent. Projected thought of the power web of
the parent planets, caught here in plus mass stasis. It
changed from pink to a watery greenish silver, and then,
achieving minus mass, it disappeared at once, the air filling the vacuum with pistol shot sound. Little Gypsy, who
now would age one year in ten. Shard stood, wishing
somberly that they had enlisted him at nineteen, rather
than at forty. Yet, at nineteen, he hadn't been ready, as
she was ready. At nineteen he would have broken, utterly. She might break, under training. He doubted it. He
had seen too many. He walked back up the tunnel, deny-
ing himself the ease of the Pack B, trying, as he walked,
to anticipate Larner's next strategem, to plan for it, to
nullify it.

CHAPTER EIGHT

Miguel Larner sat on the apron of his diorama pool, dangling his legs in the water. The Stage Three who was to be his eventual replacement lounged in a chair nearby. His name was Martin Merman and he was a bland-faced young man who, in prior life, had been an exceptionally successful guerrilla leader. His very successes had brought him to the attention of one of Miguel's predecessors.

The two men had a warm relationship, based primarily on the essential loneliness of all Stage Threes. Miguel made a point of keeping Martin Merman well versed on all current operations. Not only did it train Merman, but he often came up with quite acceptable alterations in established programs. Para-voice between them was reserved for those situations when speed of communication was essential. When there was no pressure they preferred the leisure of actual conversation.

"The Branson operation has been one of the subtler ones," Miguel said. "We couldn't handle it openly because of the possibility of interference by Shard. That's why I stepped in over a year ago and steered Enfield and Branson into handling it as a secret mission. Looked like a better chance of getting it all wound up before Shard realized it."

"How did he get onto it? Do you know?"

"When he blocked the assassination of George Fahdi, and I still insist it wasn't your fault it didn't work, he left an agent close to Smith, unfortunately a Stage Two who caught in Smith's mind the details of the pending trip to see Branson. They found they couldn't control Branson properly. That's when they made the substitution. Lorin could still snatch our fat from the fire. They tried to block him with illusions. We lost him and picked him up again at the hospital and Karen brought him here. I can get his account of the conferences published. Fahdi is the trouble point. World indignation might be just enough to tip him over."

"Won't Shard's people be hunting for this Lorin?"

"Obviously, but I suspect they know he's here where they can't touch him."

"What are you going to do then, Miguel?"

"He's finished the article. Damn good, too. As soon as I place it, I'm going to turn him loose."

"And let Shard's people pick him up and force a repudiation?"

"Exactly."

"Then what's the point of the whole thing? What is gained?"

"It's a feint, Martin. The real target is Smith."

Merman frowned and then grinned. "I see what you mean. Let Smith see his opportunity. Let him give George Fahdi a false account of the talk with Branson, now that Branson is dead, and then use his own knowledge of the *sub rosa* deal to ride into power and . . ."

"He has already given Fahdi the false account. He was quick to see the advantage after a little . . . gentle suggestion. Too bad he's a psychopathic personality. Be good material otherwise. Tough enough. Ambitious enough. Keep Shard concentrating on Lorin and maybe Fahdi can go the way of most dictators. If he's tipped over, that will put the fear of God into Stephen Chu and Garva for a time. Will of the people. All that sort of thing."

"So this Lorin becomes your stalking horse."

"Which won't please the fair Karen. Bit of an emotional set there."

"Really? It does happen sometimes. I remember a girl, back when I was a Stage Two. Talked myself into believing she could make it. Cracked up in no time at all."

"Lorin has some good latent abilities. But he won't survive Shard's gentle attentions. He's already had just about as much as he could take. There was a flaw in the substitution and he noticed it. And he can't quite bring himself to look squarely at all the inferences."

"Fahdi is prime target?"

"Like Hitler, back when I was a Stage One, Martin. That was a wild and merry chase. The Stage Three in charge arranged three assassination attempts, and each one was blocked, barely in time. Good Lord, that was nearly forty years ago."

"When you were nearly four years younger, Miguel?" Martin Merman asked gently.

"When you are a Stage One you believe in too many things. Fahdi is prime. I have three people building up the student revolt in the Argentine, several lobbying on the trade agreements at New Delhi, one teaching Garva some new and more destructive pleasures of the flesh. Those are top order. Except for this Branson thing, Shard seems to depend on those old trustworthy 'border incidents.' They're effective, but only in a limited way. Stability, unity, must come from within. That's why I've assigned so many of our people to the routine job of agricultural research—helping the actual researchers see old things in a new way. But I have a hedge against defeat, too."

"That's a nice trick if you can manage it."

"Back to the oldest continent, Martin. Back to the newest power rising in the heart of Africa in another forty, fifty years. We're stirring them up there. Making them think. Making them come alive. Like all the years of labor in India."

Martin frowned. "What would happen, Miguel, if . . . one side or the other achieved a victory so sweeping that . . . there was no turning back."

"You mean if the pot boiled over? It won't. It can't."

The soda hissed into the glass as Miguel made a drink for Dake Lorin. He handed the tall man the glass.

"Drink a toast to yourself, Dake. You get it on the front page of the *Times-News*. Bylined. Wire services all over the world."

Dake stared at him. "They wouldn't touch it when I took it to them."

"You couldn't tell them those Disservice people wouldn't raise a stink. I can. Old friends I got down there. Here's your money back. Didn't need it."

"What's your object in helping me, Mr. Larner."

Miguel shrugged his thick shoulders. "The way I work. I do you a favor. You do me a favor. That makes the world go around. Got any plans?"

"Not yet. I thought I'd see if I can't get back into the same sort of thing I was doing working for Darwin Branson. I want to see if I can get an appointment with Enfield."

"Want me to fix that?"

Dake smiled. "I guess you could, all right. I guess there isn't much you can't do. But I think I better try this on my own."

"He isn't going to be too happy when that paper hits the streets. And that ought to be in . . . about two hours."

"Think the article will do any good, Mr. Larner?"

"That kind of thing is over my head, Dake. I see it this way. Nothing will keep that dope from filtering into Brazil, North China, Irania. Of course nobody will try to keep it out of Pak-India. So the world gets to know that all the big boys were right on the verge of making a deal, and didn't quite do it. Enough people yelling and maybe it will go through anyway. Public opinion might scare the big shots. Then we'd have that free exchange of information, reopening of frontiers to air travel, cooperative use of the canals, a few disputed boundary lines redrawn to satisfy both parties. As I see it, it could work. Lloyds of Calcutta is giving seven to three on war within the next year. Maybe your article will change hell out of those odds."

"I don't think any part of it is over your head."

"I stick to my own line. Prono, and supplying the fleng joints, and the tridi franchises. Hell, so long as I can keep making a fast rupee, I should sweat up the world? I should live so long? Nice having you around, Dake. Let me know how you make out."

"You sound like a friend of mine. She has the same approximate philosophy. She calls me a do-gooder. Patrice Togelson."

"I know about her. She and me, we'd make a good team. Bring her around some time."

"She thinks she's a team all by herself. I've got to take this money back to her. She loaned it to me. To make a damn fool of myself with."

"Good luck, boy. Don't take any wooden rupees."

Dake went up and picked up his suitcase, went the rest of the way up to the lobby. He nodded at Johnny, the desk clerk, told him he was leaving for good. As he turned toward the door he heard his name called.

He turned. Karen was running toward him from the elevators. Her eyes were wide with alarm. "You're not going?"

"Yes, I am. And thanks for everything."

"But you haven't seen Miguel! He doesn't know you're going."

"I just said good-bye to him, Karen."

She half turned away from him. There was an odd expression on her face, as though she were listening for a sound that was just beyond his hearing range. Her face changed then, screwed up like the face of a child about to cry.

"Good-bye, Dake." She held her hand out. He took it.

"Good-bye, Karen."

When he was outside the door he glanced back. She stood inside, watching him through the glass. She was not standing in the casual, slumped, hoyden posture of Karen Voss. She stood slim and straight, with a sort of forlorn dignity on her face. He walked to the corner, turning once to wave. She did not respond. A charcoal-burning cab picked him up and clattered its desolate way toward the CIJ terminal. He had a twenty-minute wait for the next Philadelphia shuttle jet. The newspapers arrived barely in time. He bought two copies and took them onto the aircraft with him. Aside from two typos, the article was exactly as he had written it. And they had bannered it SECRET DEALS REVEALED, with the sub-head BRANSON'S DEPUTY IN FOUR-POWER AGREEMENT CLAIMS IRANIAN DOUBLE-CROSS SHAPING UP.

The coin was up in the air, he thought. It could land heads or tails. Heads would be a new agreement, a lessening of international tension. Tails would merely quicken the war which more than half of the world now called "inevitable."

He read it through twice, quickly, and then glanced at the rest of the news. Massacre in a religious encampment in Iowa. Fire razes abandoned plant of Youngstown Sheet and Tube. Gurkha Airforce takes long-term lease on Drew Field in Florida, in conjunction with the missile launching stations at Cocoa. Maharani kidnap attempt foiled. Skyrocketing murder statistics blamed on prono addiction, yet growers' lobby thwarts legislative control. Bigamy legalized in California after Supreme Court review. Tridi starlet found dead in bed. New North China conscription planned. Brazil develops deadly virus mutation. New soil deficiency isolated at Kansas lab. Texas again threatens secession. Enfield KeyWesting.

Dake frowned as he read the last item. With the publication of his article, he would be poison to anyone except Enfield himself, and perhaps with him too, but at least it was a chance. There were a few more minutes of the flight left. During the last two days he had come to avoid all introspective moments, to busy his mind with activity —any kind of activity—just so it kept him from thinking.

Stream of thought was like a swift river that ran smoothly down a channel and then broke suddenly against a rock. That rock was the flaw he had seen in Branson, and the manner of his "death." After striking the rock, the current boiled into an eddy, circling aimlessly. A thousand times he had tried to dismiss it by telling himself that he was mistaken. Auto-hypnosis. A tiny flaw in the mind, a wrinkle resulting from strain. For the first time in many days he thought consciously of his wife. The dull feeling of loss lingered always in his subconscious, ready to be brought to the surface. A quiet, bright-eyed girl who had loved him. There had been for a long time an inability to believe that she was dead. He would meet her around the next corner. Maybe the strain had started when he had at last faced the fact that she was utterly and incredibly gone. Wife and father—and both, somehow, killed by different aspects of the same thing. Father killed by a small corruption, and wife by a vaster one—yet the difference was only in degree.

These, he thought, were poor years for a constructive idealist. The dream was always the same. Do a little bit, to the limit of your strength, and it will become a better world, after you have gone. If each man does a little bit . . . Maybe, back in the eighteen hundreds that dream had a little validity. Men could believe, back there, that the world became a little bit better each year. But then, following the first two world wars, the dream had somehow become reversed. Men of good will began to believe that the world was getting worse. Thought became nihilistic, or existentialistic. Praise the gods of nothingness.

Yet somehow there had been more vitality in thinking the world was getting worse than in the tepid philosophizings of the middle sixties when it was believed that the world never gets better or worse—it remains always on an even keel of disorder, Christ played off against Dachau, with the game always ending in a draw. A bad time for functional idealism. Patrice and Miguel were the inevitable products of the culture. Let me get mine—fast.

How much simpler to fall into their way of life. The devil take my grandchildren. Corruption is always with us. The game always ends in a draw, and all the efforts of one man cannot affect that immutable decision.

Patrice provided the easy doorway. She had always urged him to come in with her. "There are so many things you could do, darling. I need someone to handle public relations, to deal with some of my compadres who seem to resent dealing with a woman. Some of the Indians look at me as though they thought I should be in purdah. I could pay you well, but it wouldn't be charity or a gift or anything, because I *do* need you."

Not quite yet, Patrice. Not until I can recognize the

inevitability of defeat. And maybe I'll never recognize that.

As the aircraft dipped over Philadelphia he saw that there had been another one of the power failures which seemed to become more frequent each year. Angular sections of the city were blacked out. Nobody screamed with outraged indignation anymore. With enough technicians, money and standby equipment, there would be no power failures. But Philadelphia, as all other cities, lacked all three factors. Standard correctional procedure was to appoint a committee to look into the findings of the committee which had been appointed to make a survey. The answer was always the same. We lack oil and coal and ore and copper and zinc and tin and timber and men.

He caught a cab, had to transfer to another when the first one broke down. He felt uneasy riding through the dark streets with the money in his wallet. Philadelphia was infested with child gangs. The dissolution and decay of the school system had put them on the streets. They had the utter, unthinking ruthlessness of children in all ages. The guerrilla days had filled the land with weapons. Put an antique zip gun in the hands of an eleven-year-old child from a prono-saturated home, and you had an entity which thought only in terms of the pleasing clatter of the gun itself, with imagination so undeveloped as yet that the adults who were ripped by the slugs were not creatures capable of feeling pain, but merely exciting symbols of an alien race. They were like the children he had read about who had lived in caves in the rubble of Berlin after the Second World War.

He got out of the cab in front of Patrice's house, saw the lights and felt secure again. The cab drove away as he started up the walk. The faint movement of a shadow among shadows startled him. He saw it from the corner of his eye. He turned quickly, saw nothing. He waited for a few moments and then turned toward the house. The pretty Japanese maid opened the door and gave him her usual welcoming smile, glinting with gold.

"Good evening, Mr. Lor——"

He had stepped into the hall. She stared at him and her

face changed, grotesquely. She put one hand to her throat. She took a step backward and her eyes bulged in a glassy way as though, at last, after years of nightmare, she now faced the ultimate horror.

"What's wrong with you?"

She took another step and suddenly crumpled, to lie still on the hall rug. He leaned over her. Patrice came out into the hall.

"Dake! What on earth happened to Molly?"

"I don't know. She just stared at me and looked horrified and fainted. I guess it's a faint."

Patrice knelt by the small frail figure, began to rub her wrist, pat her wan cheek. "Molly! Molly dear!"

She frowned and then glanced up at Dake. "I don't know what——" She stopped and stared at him intently, and her face suddenly looked like chalk. "God," she whispered softly. "God!" She shut her eyes tightly, squinching up her face. She swayed on her knees as though she would topple over the figure of the maid.

"What's wrong!" Dake demanded. "What is it?"

She kept her eyes shut. "I don't want to . . . look. It's . . . your face."

Dake instinctively lifted his hand to touch his face. He rubbed his left cheek with his right hand. It felt completely normal. He ran his hand across his mouth and suddenly stopped, his heart thudding. He gingerly touched his right cheek, his fingertips making a whispering sound against the hard polished bone. He slid his fingertips up to touch the empty ivory eye socket.

He reached the big hall mirror in three strides and stared at himself. Had a polished skull-head stared back at him it would not have been anywhere near as horrible as to see the face evenly divided between life and death. One side flushed, warm, alive. On the other side the naked teeth.

Impossibility!

Face to face with all the myriad logical answers. None of them logical. Take half a man's face off and he bleeds to death. He looked into the mirror and saw, behind him, the reflected image of Patrice, her face in her hands, kneeling beside the still form of Molly—the little maid who had been so proud of learning the syllable *L* that she had changed her name.

He saw a cliff in the back of his mind, and sanity clung, scrabbling with bleeding fingers, to the sheer edge. Easier to drop into nothingness, turning over and over through the endless fall. Easier to scream and giggle and destroy the two women with murderous fear.

He walked slowly to a position behind Patrice, looked down on her shining head.

His voice sounded rusty. "Would you ever try to tell anyone about this?"

"No. No!"

"Then how many others have seen things . . . like this, and knew they dared not speak of them, Patrice?"

"What are you trying to say?"

"Are we dreaming this? Is it happening? Are you the Patrice of my dreams?"

"You're . . . in my dream, Dake. In my nightmare."

"How do we go about waking up?"

"You know we're awake," she whispered. "What . . . are you?"

"A beastie? A demon? I'm Dake. I don't understand it any better than you do. Look at me."

"No."

He took the shining hair in his fist and wrenched her head back. "Look at me!" She moaned, but kept her eyes tight shut. With his free hand he thumbed back her eyelid, even as she clawed at his wrist. She did not move or breathe. The wide eye stared at him. She screamed then. A scream that tore his nerves. That final utter scream of the last panic. She jumped and spun away, staring at him, still screaming, pausing only to fill her lungs and scream again. And stopped. And stood in the echoing silence and began to laugh, bending and twisting and holding herself with laughter, running then, doubling over with laughter, running against the door and rebounding to run again and at last tearing it open, running out into the night, laughing, tripping, falling, lying there in the diagonal of light from the open door, her legs still making spasmodic running motions, her laughter sounding as though her throat were slowly filling with blood. . . .

He understood. Her bold proud mind had been full of arrogance, of certainty, of the knowledge of infallibility. Faced with the hideous and inexplicable, the mind had been unable to bend, unable to accept impossibility. And so, under strain, it had broken clearly, cleanly. Her example oddly gave him an understanding of how close he was to the same fracture line, gave him that necessary increment of pliability that kept him from breaking.

He knew that they would bring her back, quickly perhaps, to a relative sanity. But that new sanity would be a weak patch on the broken mind. She would walk in uncertainty, with the morbid expectation that around the very next corner she might find . . . a new inexplicable horror.

Molly, the Japanese maid, was a different case. Here was no proud and rigid mind, dependent on an explicable world. Here was a willingness to accept the unknown on its own terms. It would give her bad night dreams. It would give her delicious chills from time to time. But she would not break through the necessity of having to find a reason for something that was without reason.

They came, the obsequious and silken little doctors of the very rich, murmuring their concern, manicured fingers timing the flutter of pulse, phoning in subdued voices for the very best of hospital suites, the most accomplished of private nurses, and making the deft quieting injections, cautioning the attendants who levered the still Viking body into the chrome and gold of the huge Taj ambulance for the hushed flight through the night streets of the city.

One doctor rode with the sleeping woman, and the other, with many nervous glances at his watch, questioned Dake and Molly. Dake had known from the vaguely irritable glances the doctors had given him that his face was no longer horror. He had furtively fingered his cheek to make certain.

Molly sat in a straight chair, her fists propped rigid atop her thighs, her ankles neatly together, the black hair drawn back tightly, sheening oiled blue and green in the lamplight. Her eyes would flick toward Dake, slide uneasily away.

"It seems," the doctor said, "to be a form of hysteria. It may help the diagnosis, Mr. Lorin, if you would tell me the apparent cause."

"I was only here a few moments before it happened, Doctor. I flew down from New York this evening, and taxied out here."

"When you first saw her did she seem upset in any way?"

Dake was laughing inwardly. It was unpleasant laughter. Try to tell this neat fussy little man the truth and he would have you wrapped up and labeled for delivery to one of the state institutions, despite the shortage of beds and treatment for the insane. The spiraling curve of psychosis during the past fifteen years had altered the admission requirements. Potential violence seemed to be the only remaining criterion. The milder species of manic-depressive, psychopathic personalities, schizos, paranoids —all roamed the streets, lost in their ritualistic fantasies. There had been a rebirth of that dark ages belief that to give money to the mad is one of the doorways to grace. Membership in the most marginal cults was, to many, an accepted release for obsession.

"She did not seem upset," Dake said. "It seemed to happen quickly."

The doctor turned to Molly. "Has she been herself lately?"

"Yes, sir." Soft voice that trembled.

He looked at the maid and knew she would say nothing. The doctor sighed and looked at his watch again. "You aren't much help, either of you. Miss Togelson has always impressed me as a very strong personality. This is rather . . . shocking, from a personal point of view. Neither of you know what she meant with all that babbling about skulls?"

Dake saw the maid shudder. He said, "Sorry, no."

"I'll be off then."

"Could you give me a lift, Doctor, if you're heading downtown?"

"Come along."

As they went onto the porch Dake heard the maid slide the locks on the big door. As they got into the car he saw the lights coming on in room after room. Molly would want a lot of light around her. She would want the night to be like day.

The doctor drove with reckless casual impatience. "Where are you going, Mr. Lorin?"

"I checked luggage at the CIJ downtown terminal."

"I'll drop you at the door."

"Can I phone you tomorrow to find out about Miss Togelson?"

"In the afternoon."

The doctor let him out and started up almost before Dake had slammed the car door. He went into the brightly lighted terminal. Two large groups of Indian tourists were chatting, laughing. Their women wore saris heavily worked with gold and silver. They gave him a quick incurious glance. They came from a hard, driving, ambitious and wealthy land. It was fashionable to tour the bungling rattle-trap Western world. So quaint, my dear. But the people! So incredibly lethargic. And so excitingly vulgar. Naturally we owe them a debt—I mean this is the country where modern mass production methods originated, you know. In fact, we used to import their technicians, send our young people to their engineering schools. Think of it! But of course we've improved tremendously on all of their techniques. Tata set up the first completely automated steel mill. I suppose the war *did* exhaust these people terribly. We don't know how lucky we are that Pak-India has never been a bomb target. And we're strong enough so that it never will be. You heard President Lahl's latest speech, of course. Any overt act will be punished a thousandfold. That made Garva and Chu and Fahdi sit up and take notice.

CHAPTER NINE

Dake took his luggage to a nearby hotel, registered, had a late supper and went up to his room. He was unpacking his toilet articles when the bellhop arrived with the typewriter.

"It doesn't look like much, sir, but the assistant manager says it's in good shape." He carried it over to the desk by the window and set it down.

"I didn't order a typewriter sent up."

The bellhop was a chinless and earnest young man. He gave Dake an uneasy smile. "I suppose that's some kind of a joke, Mr. Lorin. I guess I don't get it."

"What do you mean?"

"Well, I was in here ten minutes ago when you sent for a boy, and you told me you wanted a typewriter. I mean, if it's a gag, I don't get it."

Before the episode with Patrice, Dake knew he would have objected strenuously. He would have phoned the manager and asked if this was a new method of gouging the guests. He would have demanded that the typewriter be taken away.

But the world was altering in some obscure way. A brassy little wench had talked imaginatively of the delusion of reality. Half a death's head in a mirror. A woman mad from fright. A fingernail. Fundamentally he was a man of curiosity. A reporter. He could not ignore the objective questions triggered by subjective experience.

He tipped the boy. "Not a very good joke, I guess."

The boy sighed. "Thanks, sir. You had me worried there for a minute. I wondered if I was going nuts. Good night, sir."

86

The boy closed the door after him. Dake stood in the middle of the room, rubbing his chin. This, like every other damnable thing that had happened, had two aspects. The other side of the coin was that he *had* requested a typewriter. Insanity. Delusion. But Molly and Patrice had seen something. Could that be objective proof? Only, he thought, if he could prove to himself that he had gone to her house and what he imagined had happened had actually happened. He went quickly to the phone. It took twenty minutes to get the hospital. Phone service had changed over the years from a convenience to an annoying irritant.

The girl at the hospital switchboard answered at last.

"Do you have a patient there, recently admitted? A Miss Patrice Togelson?"

"Just a moment, sir. I'll check."

He waited. She came back on the line and said, "Yes sir. She was admitted about three hours ago. She is resting comfortably, sir."

"Thank you."

He hung up, sat on the edge of the bed, lit a cigarette. All right. Take it another step. How do I prove I made that call, and prove I talked to the girl at the hospital switchboard? The call will appear on my bill. Yet, when I see it noted on the bill, how do I know I am actually seeing it?

There was a stabbing pain centered behind his eyes, a pain so sudden and intense that it blinded him. He closed his eyes and opened them again, aware of an abrupt transition, aware that time had passed. Instead of being seated on the bed, he was seated in front of the desk. A dingy sheet of hotel stationery was rolled into the typewriter. Several lines had been typed.

Dake read them mechanically. "To whom it may concern: When Darwin Branson died I saw that I could use his death to my own advantage. I saw a way I could put myself back in the public eye. I had worked for Darwin Branson for a full year, but his assigned task had been to make a detailed survey of State Department policy decisions. He was not engaged in any way in secret negotiations.

"The article I wrote for the *Times-News* was a ruse. No such agreements were made. I had the plan of writing the article in order to help promote world unity. I realize now that it was a delusion of grandeur. I realize now that the article will have the reverse effect from what I had planned. I feel that at the time I wrote the article I was not responsible for my actions.

"The only way I can make amends is to write this full confession and then proceed to . . ."

It stopped there. The sudden time transition seemed to leave him numbed, unable to comprehend. The words seemed meaningless. He moved his lips as he read it again, much like a child trying to comprehend an obscure lesson in a textbook.

"No!" he said thickly.

The pain again focused behind his eyes, but not as intensely as before. It was almost as though it were coming to him through some shielding substance. It made his vision swim, but it did not black him out entirely. There was a pulsating quality to it, a strength that increased and diminished, as though in conflict.

He tried to keep his hands at his sides, but they lifted irresistibly to the keys of the typewriter. A new word. ". . . take . . ."

He held his hands rigid. Sweat ran down the side of his throat. Two hard clacks as his fingers hit the keys. ". . . my . . ."

The feeling of combat in his mind, of entities battling for control, was sharp and clear. He did not feel that he was fighting with any strength. He was something limp, helpless, being pushed and pulled at the same time.

". . . own . . ."

His hands flexed, the knuckles crackling.

". . . life."

And again, without temporal hiatus, his pen was in his hand, his signature already scrawled at the foot of the sheet, the sheet out of the typewriter. Blackout, and he was at the window, one long leg over the sill, the window

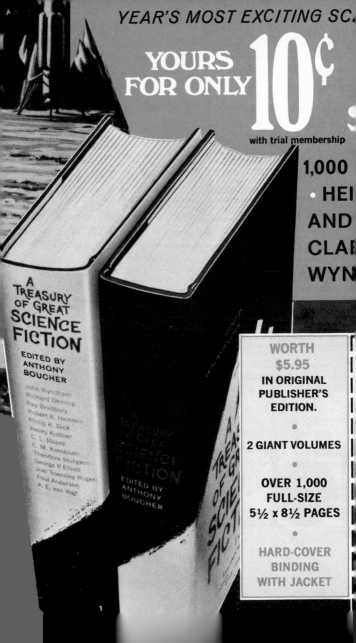

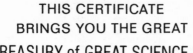

flung high, sharp October night breathing against his face, an enclosed court far below, a few lighted windows across from him, like watchful eyes.

Conflict crescendoed in his mind and was suddenly gone. Emptiness. He straddled the sill, motionless. No more pushing and pulling. Easy now to let go. Easier than trying to find answers to problems. Easier than fighting insanity. Let go and spin slowly down through the whispering night, down by the lighted windows, down to that final answer. He heard himself make a sniggling sound, a drunken giggle. He sensed the impending rupture of his brain. A bursting of tissues. His hand tightened on the sill. Come now, God of darkness. Take your tired child. Find the dark land father, hanging in the stone cell of eternity, turning slowly with blackened face. Find the wife who one instant was warmth, and now lives forever in the heart of the whiteness hotter than the sun.

But . . . WHY?

Drop with question unanswered? Fall to the smash of bone on stone and never know why?

His mind wheeled for one insane instant and focused on WHY. Big letters, the color of flame, written on the black night. Never knowing was more horrid than continuing the conflict, the distortion of reality.

He released his hold and fell into the room, fell with a slack-muscled helplessness, his head thudding on the rug. He lay on his back and grasped his hard thighs with long-fingered hands, sensing the fibrous nerves, meaty tissues, churn of blood. He tasted his aliveness with his hands, content not to think for a little while. The drapery moved with the night wind. The wind cooled the sweat on his face. He heard the faraway city sound. Not like the roaring burly sounds of the old days. The cities had thinner sounds now. A lost and lonely scream was a part of each night.

Dake sat up slowly, feeling as though hallucination had drained his strength. He hitched closer to the window, wanting to close it. The sash was out of his reach, yet he did not quite dare stand to reach it. He hitched over, stood up, leaning against the wall. He reached one hand over, blindly, slid the sash down with a shattering bang. He turned his heavy shoulders against the wall.

In front of him was an evanescence, the faintest silvery shimmer. It was much like that first warning flicker of migraine, dread shining blindness.

And Karen Voss stood there, brown hair tousled, thumb tucked pertly in the wide belt, luminous gray eyes full of pale concern and sassy arrogance. He drew his lips back flat against his teeth and made a small sick sound in his throat and tried to reassure himself by passing his hard arm through the vision. His wrist struck the warm roundness of her shoulder, staggering her.

"Don't try to explain things to yourself," she said quickly. Her voice was tense. "Got to get you out of here." She stepped quickly to the desk, snatched up the typed confession, ripped it quickly. She looked over her shoulder at him. "I hate to think of how many credits I'm losing. Start drooling and babbling and prove I'm wrong."

Dake straightened his shoulders. "Go straight to hell," he said thickly.

She studied him for a moment, head tilted to one side. She took his wrist, warm fingers tightening, pulling him toward the door. "I remember how you must feel. I'll break some more rules, now that I've started. You're expected to go mad, my friend. Just keep remembering that. And don't."

At the door she paused. "Now do exactly as I say. Without question. I kept you from going out that window."

"What do you want?"

"We're going to try to get out of here. The competition is temporarily . . . kaput. If we get separated, go to Miguel. You understand? As quickly as you can."

He felt her tenseness as they went down all the flights of stairs to the lobby, went out into the night. "Now walk fast," she said.

Down the block, around the corner, over to Market. She pulled him into a dark shallow doorway.

"What are we . . ."

"Be still." She stood very quietly. In the faint light of a

distant streetlamp he could see that her eyes were half shut.

Suddenly she sighed. "The competition is no longer kaput, Dake. They've got an idea of direction."

An ancient car meandered down the potholed street, springs banging, engine making panting sounds. It swerved suddenly and came over to the curb and stopped. A gaunt, raw-looking man stepped out, moving like a puppet with an amateur handling the strings. He went off down the sidewalk, lifting his feet high with each step.

"Get in and drive it," Karen said, pushing impatiently at him. He cramped his long legs under the wheel. She got in beside him. He drove down the street, hearing behind them the frantic yawp of the dispossessed driver.

She called the turns. They entered an area of power failure, as dark as one of the abandoned cities.

"Stop here and we'll leave the car," she said.

They walked down the dark street. She stepped into an almost invisible alley mouth. "Wait," she said.

Once again she was still. He heard her long sigh. "Nothing in range, Dake. Come on. North Seventh is a couple of blocks over. Bright lights. Crowds. That's the best place."

"It's a bad place to go. For a couple."

"We're safe, Dake."

"What did you do to that man in the car?"

She didn't answer. Her high heels clacked busily in double time to his long stride. They came to streetlights again. Brown hair bounced against the nape of her neck as she walked.

"What did you people do to Branson?"

Again she refused to answer.

"If you *are* people," he said with surly emphasis. "I don't care about your . . . motivations. I won't forgive what was done to Patrice."

"Please shut up. Stop grumbling."

Two men appeared suddenly out of the shadows, a dozen paces ahead. Dake stopped at once, turned and glanced quickly behind them, saw the others there, heard the odd whinnying giggle of a mind steeped in prono, anticipating the sadist fury. Karen had kept on walking. He caught her in two strides, hand yanking on her shoulder.

She spun out of his grasp. He gasped and stared at the two men. They had turned into absurd dolls, leaping stiff-legged in grotesque dance, bellowing in fright and pain. One rebounded off the front of a building, caught crazy balance and rebounded again. The other pitched headlong into the gutter and rolled onto his back and began banging his heels against the pavement, arching his back. Dake could think of nothing but insects which had blundered into a cone of light which had blinded them, bewildered them, driven them frantic with heat and pain. Behind them the other men bounded and bucked and sprawled. Karen did not change her pace. He caught up with her. She gave him a sidelong gamin grin, a squint of ribald humor in the glow of streetlights.

"Dance of the pronies," she said.

"And there is no point, I suppose, in asking you . . . what did that?"

"Why not? A headache. A rather severe one. It gave them something to think about. Like this."

He staggered and clapped his palm hard over the lance of pure flame that ran from temple to temple, a rivulet of fire. It stopped his breath for a moment. And it was gone as quickly as it had come. There was lingering pain. But the memory of pain was almost as hurtful as the pain itself.

She took his hand. "You'd be much more difficult, Dake. Prono makes mush of them. Soft, sticky little brains. Like wet glue. We'll go over there to that place. A breathing spell. I've got to think how I can get us back to New York."

The fleng joint was a slow cauldron of mass desperation. Prone and fice, and fleng strip routines, and the gut-roil of the kimba music, and the rubbery walls like white wet flesh. During the Great Plague in London, man, obsessed by dissolution, had made an earnest attempt to rejoin the slime from which he had once come. Now the plague was of the spirit, and the effect was the same. They pushed their way through to a lounging table, and waved away the house clowns, refused a cubicle ticket, managed to order native whiskey. She put her lips, with their heavy makeup, close to his ear.

"We're going to separate here, Dake. That will be the best way. I could try to help you get to Miguel, but they can find me easier than they can you. I'll be more harm than help."

"And if I don't want to get to Miguel?"

"Don't be such a fool. It isn't a case of wanting. If you don't get there, you'll die. Maybe you want to do that. If you want to die, then I'm wrong about you."

He turned toward her and saw the sudden panic change her face. Though her lips did not move, and he was certain she had not spoken, her words were clear in his mind, coming with a rapidity that speech could not have duplicated.

"I didn't do as well as I thought: A Stage Three picked us up. Coming in the door over there. The man with the long red hair. I'm going to distract him. Leave as quickly as you can and don't pay any attention to anything. Understand? Anything! No matter how crazy it looks to you. Go to Miguel as quickly as you can and . . . be careful when you get there. You'll be safe once you're in the lobby. But the street out in front will be dangerous. Be very careful. Go now. Hurry!"

He slid from the table and plunged toward the door. A small man with a wooden look on his face hopped up onto one of the show platforms and dived at the sick-looking man with the long red hair. A woman screeched and raced at the red-haired man. Dake felt a surge of terror so strong that he knew, somehow, that it had been induced in his brain by Karen to give him more speed, more energy.

The red-haired man was twisting in a knot of people who oddly fell away from him, as though all interest in him were suddenly lost. Dake burst through the door and found himself running with others. Running with a pack of others. And he saw that they were all himself. He saw a dozen Dake Lorins bursting from the door, running in all directions, and he screamed as he ran, screamed and

looked back over his shoulder as he screamed, saw the
red-haired one stand on the sidewalk and then topple as
someone dived against his legs. He ran silently then, lifting his long legs, running until white pain burned his side
and scorched his lungs. He slowed and walked, struggling
for breath, his knees fluttering, sweat cold on his body.

The cabdriver was reluctant. He said he didn't make
trips like that. He yielded to two arguments—Dake's
strangling arm across his throat and the thousand-rupee
note in front of his eyes. Dake took the man's gun and
shoved it inside his belt. Dawn wasn't far away as they
turned into the only tunnel to Manhattan that had not become flooded and unusable through neglect. In the city
the white police trucks were collecting the bodies of those
who had died violently in the night. Dake felt caked and
dull and old, worn dry with emotional hangover. They
went through the dark streets in those predawn hours
when life is at its lowest ebb—the hours of aimless re-
grets, of the sense of waste, of the knowledge of death.
The October stars wheeled in a corrosive indifference to
all the works of man. The city slept . . . restlessly.

CHAPTER TEN

Mindful of Karen's last warning, he had the driver stop two blocks from the above-ground lobby of the apartment dwelling where Miguel lived. He gave the man the thousand-rupee note, returned his gun. The man gave him a surly nod, made a screeching U-turn, reckless of his precious tires, drive back downtown, single red eye blinking as the rough road surface joggled a loose connection.

Dake moved with instinctive animal caution, staying on the darker side of the street, stepping lightly and quickly through patches of faint radiance. The above-ground lobby was lighted. He could see the head of the desk clerk bent over a book on the high desk. The soft light of the lobby made a semicircle of radiance that reached almost to the midpoint of the road.

Dake waited for a time in the shadows, oddly restless, and then walked out boldly, heading directly across the street for the doors. His heels were loud on the asphalt. He heard a faint scuffing noise in the shadows behind him and to his left. He did not turn, but lengthened his stride. The area of light was two steps away. He took another long stride and was caught there, motionless. Something had clamped down on volition, something that held him as though, in an instant, he had been turned to ice, or stone. He could not change even the direction of his sight. The clerk was just off his center of vision. He saw the head lift abruptly. He moved then, taking a long step backward with infinite unwilled stealth. Another step.

Miguel Larner appeared suddenly, just inside the doors. Dake had not seen where he had come from, or how. The man wore a pair of florid pajamas. He stood very still. A stranger appeared behind him, another beside him, and a tall woman appeared over near the desk. The five persons inside the bright lobby stood and watched him. They were fifty feet away. He could see no expression on their faces, but their eyes seemed bright, feral. He was aware of how alien they were. They emanated a tangible coldness.

Something behind him was frightened. He could taste fright that nibbled at the edges of his mind. A hard compression of force erupted into his brain. It sucked him forward, running with a vast awkwardness, a shamble-legged, slack-armed lunge that took him stumbling across the sidewalk, diving for the doors that flicked open barely in time, to let him slide and roll on the slick floor, to thud against the base of the desk as the woman stepped lightly out of the way. He sat up. They had all moved closer to the door. They filed out and stood in a row on the sidewalk. On the far side of the street something flounced and rolled and made guttural sounds in the darkness. They all came back in. Miguel Larner came over to Dake. His eyes were vast and hung in pure velvet blackness, unsupported. There was nothing else in the world but the eyes of Miguel Larner. Little fingers pried under the edge of Dake's soul and flipped him. He fell off the edge into blackness.

It was a cloudless spring morning by Miguel's dioramic pool. Dake shut his eyes again. He remembered a time long ago. Eight years old. He had seen the overhead lights of the operating room. Then heard a hollow echoing voice in his head, saying, as though in a long tunnel, "mmmm-*gas!* mmmmm-*gas!* mmmmm-*GAS!*"

And then the bleary awakening—the over-large faces of his parents looking down at him on the bed—big faces suspended at odd angles. "How do you feel?" A voice that echoed down a long empty tunnel.

He opened his eyes again. He was on a gay beach chair by the pool. Miguel and a stranger looked at him with that cold sobriety, that extra-human speculation he had seen in the lobby—how long ago? A year, or a minute.

Miguel's lips moved. "Mr. Lorin. Mr. Merman."

"How do you do." Dake wanted to let loose crazy laughter at the quaintness of the formality. He trapped the laughter in his throat.

Merman had a boy's face, an old man's eyes.

"You did well," Miguel said, "to get in range of Johnny. Otherwise Karen's rather pathetic little exhibition of stubbornness would have been quite pointless. They've brought her in. She wants to see you. I'll call her. Don't speak to her."

No answer seemed necessary. Miguel gave Merman a quick sharp look and nodded. Dake had the idea they were communicating with each other. Karen came out to the pool, stood on the apron at the far side of the pool and looked at Dake. He was shocked at the change in her. Her face was wan and pinched, and her eyes were enormous. Her mouth had a trembling, old-lady uncertainty about it, and her fingers plucked at the edges of her grubby skirt. Two things seemed mingled inextricably in her eyes. A keen, warm, personal interest in him, and also a look of confused dullness—the look sometimes seen in the eyes of a dog beaten once too often.

Miguel nodded at her and she turned and left, walking aimlessly, shaking her head, saying something to herself that Dake could not understand.

"What happened to her?" Dake asked.

"I'll tell you, but just remember it, don't try to understand it. Later . . . if you are more than I think you are, understanding will catch up with you. Remember this. Two screens badly torn. The third screen bruised. She'll be a long time healing, relearning, readjusting. She'll be a long time here, Dake Lorin."

"What is this all about?" Dake asked. He had a sense of futility as he asked the question. Miguel Larner went over to the pool, sat and dangled his legs in the water, his bare brown back toward Dake. Dake looked toward the young-old face of Merman. His eyes veered suddenly toward something that had moved on the stones of the terrace. A tiny column of little naked savage figures snake-danced their way toward his ankles. Four-inch figures with animal faces. Their tiny cries were like the cries of insects. He instinctively snatched his feet up into the chair. They swarmed up the chair legs.

The memory of Karen's voice came to him across present horror. "You're expected to go mad, my friend. Just keep remembering that. And don't."

He shut his eyes and slowly lowered his feet to the floor. He felt them running across his clothing, plucking at him, prodding, pinching. They clambered up his chest, up his face, entangled tiny fists in his hair and swung themselves up. He opened his eyes and he was in utter blackness. He was naked. A long cold something coiled its way slowly across his foot. He set his teeth in his lower lip and did not cry out or move. He fell to hot bright yellow sand. Fat spiders skittered across the sand. He looked more closely and saw that they were dismembered human hands, standing tall and agile on plump fingers, circling him with quick darts of movement. Two of them struggled toward him, dragging something, dragging, he saw, Karen's head, the spider fingers scrubbling in the sand with the effort. A shadow crossed him. He turned and looked up, squinting at a featureless sky. Something hung there. A figure so huge that it reduced him to the size of an insect. A rope encircled its neck, extending out of sight into the sky. The huge figure turned slowly. He looked up into the purpling bloated face of his father. He turned, ready to run whooping through all the yellow sand of eternity, ready to run with bulged eyes until blood burst his throat. He dropped to his knees on the sand. He covered his eyes. He sensed the ancient brain scar, felt it swell and tear slightly and then knit itself, fiber clasping fiber, compacting into strength. He stood up and turned and looked calmly up at the vast naked face. Spiders scuttled off into the sand waste. Coils moved off into darkness. The bitter little insect squeakings faded into an utter silence.

Miguel's bare brown back appeared and the sand faded around it, faded into terrace and pool and the still spring morning of the diorama.

Miguel turned and looked at him over the brown

shoulder, smiled. "It seems I must be proven wrong occasionally."

"I'll never break," Dake said, not knowing why he had selected those words.

"Merman will show you the way."

He followed Merman. The rock slid aside. The glowing tunnel shafted down through bedrock. Three cubes of a fatty gray that was no color at all stood in a rough cavern hollowed out of the rock. The radiance in the cavern had an almost radioactive look.

Merman turned to Dake. The boyish lips did not move. "You are going to a place where you will be trained. You will accept training eagerly, because you want to turn it against us. That is to be expected. You wonder what we are. You will not learn that until you are skilled."

An orifice slit opened in the side of one of the ten-foot cubes. He edged through the opening. The cube, except for a small triple row of studs near the opening, was featureless. Merman reached through the opening, touched a stud, stepped back quickly. The slit closed. Light came through the cube walls. He looked at Merman as though looking through water. Long ago, in his mother's kitchen, he had delighted in using an object called an egg slicer. Place a hardboiled egg in the cupped place, and pull the handle down slowly. Tiny wires sliced through the egg.

This was that egg slicer, and it happened in the space of a tenth of a heartbeat. A billion wires. Each one sliced neatly through his body. The pain Karen had given him was, by comparison, a tiny pinch, a nip of the flesh.

And the pain was gone, the orifice partially open. His one desire was to get out of that cube as quickly as humanly possible. He was caught in the yielding slit for a moment, and then tumbled free, thinking he was on the floor of the cavern. A sky of such a pallid blue as to be almost white burned overhead, deepening in color toward the horizons. He was on hands and knees on a featureless metallic plain. Around him was a matrix of the gray cubes arranged in painfully perfect geometric design, all joined by gleaming metal tubes. His cube was joined to its neighbors, as were the others. He stood up, and his feet left the metallic surface in an awkward little jump. Here and there cubes were missing from the pattern, leaving the tube ends raw and naked. It was oddly disturbing to see the design incomplete, as though looking at a lovely woman with several front teeth missing.

Low against the horizon off to his right two small moons hung clear in the sky, one slightly larger than the other. The sun overhead had a redness about it that altered the shadows of the cubes and tubes, giving them a burned look.

Far across the metallic plain rose the gigantic trees of childhood, and near the bases of them, dwarfed by their size, he could see the low black buildings to which he must walk. He knew he had to go there. He did not know how he knew. It had the inevitability of a dream compulsion. Strangely, he felt acceptance in him. This was not his world. This was not his planet or his system. He knew that if night came he would see unthinkable constellations. He threaded his way through the geometric maze of cubes, stepping over the low tubes that joined them. He came to the open plain and walked toward the buildings. He tried to hurry and found that the best pace was a long gliding step. There was no ⌐ bellion, no questioning of reality. He was *here* and it was very necessary to get to the black buildings, and very necessary to learn what had to be learned, and acquire the skills that must be acquired. There would be only one chance.

They came out of the buildings and he was but mildly aware of his own odd lack of curiosity about them. There was merely a sense that some of them were learning, as he would learn, and some of them taught, and some of them ran the machines for teaching.

All of them, men and women, and the odd-looking non-men, and non-woman, wore only heavy skirt-like garments that extended to mid-thigh. They chattered in strange tongues, and some spoke awkward English, and some spoke good English. He was herded quickly into a room, stripped, scorched with a harsh spray of some astringent liquid, given a garment and hurried along into another place where he was measured by a pair of violet-eyed non-women, whose faces were subtly wrong, whose movements were curiously articulated in a quite unexpected fashion. He knew, somehow, that it was measurement that they did. As they swung the little burring heads of the glowing equipment down over his body, as he felt the chitter and nibbling, and saw the smooth gray plates dropping into the trough near the wall, he sensed that every grain, fiber and atom of him was being measured and remembered and recorded. He cooperated like an automaton. Like a man who has gone to the same barber for so many years that he has learned to move his head to exactly the right angle at exactly the right time. He suffered the wheel and blackout of the ribbands that encircled his head, the electronic cluckings of the little plates that sucked against his temples.

Cleaned and dressed and measured and recorded and remembered, he was sent alone down a corridor. He turned in at an open doorway, knowing that it was the right doorway. The door banged down behind him like a guillotine, and automatonism left him at once. He guessed that it was a feeling of suddenly being released from post-hypnotic influence. There was the same fear, the same uncertainty.

The girl stared at him. She had dark tangled hair, broken fingernails, a hard bold bright light in her eyes. Her garment was a livid orange that went well with the slender brown of her dusky body. The room walls were cocoa brown, rounded at the corners, featureless. There was light, without visible light source.

She spoke to him in a harsh tongue, her voice rising at the end of the phrase in a question.

He shook his head. "I don't understand." She tried again, slowly. He shrugged. She made an obscene gesture with her hands, spat on the floor toward his feet, turned her back.

He stared at the simple furnishings of the sealed room, the rigid cots, the two chairs, the single table.

"You have been placed together because you cannot understand each other's language."

The voice seemed to have its origin inside his head. He saw the girl wheel, look for the source of the voice, and he knew that she heard it too.

"This room is so constructed that it aids the projection and reception of thought. When you have learned to give your thoughts to each other, you will find that together you can open the door."

The voice stopped. They looked speculatively at each other. He looked into her eyes and tried to will her to go to the table and sit at one of the chairs. He made the command clear in his mind. She was staring hard at him. She suddenly shrugged and turned away, and he guessed that she had been trying to will some message into his brain. He had neither projected nor received. It was going to be far more difficult than he had imagined. He tried to think of some simple way they could experiment.

At last he took her arm and pulled her over to one of the chairs. She sat down, scowling at him, obviously disliking being touched. He sat in the other chair so that they faced each other across the table. He bit off a sizable fragment of fingernail, showed it to her. She looked puzzled. He put his hands behind him, transferred it to his left hand, and then placed both fists on the table.

"Left," he thought. "Left hand."

She reached out and tentatively touched his left hand. He showed her the bit of nail and she beamed at him, clapped her hands. Then, after many more attempts, they both became depressed. She was correct six out of ten times, then seven out of twelve, and then eleven out of twenty. He tried each time to push the thought into her mind. It was much like being under water and trying to push against a huge stone. One could kick weakly, but there was no pivot place. No place to brace the feet. No way to put force behind the effort.

He was pleased to see that she had a determination and tenacity that matched his own. Her small jaw was set hard with the effort. She took the fragment of nail and tried. He strained to hear her thoughts, found that he was only guessing, operating solely on hunches. They worked at it with stubborn energy until they were exhausted. His

despair was transformed into anger at her. He could not
succeed because they had given him this fool girl. Anyone
else but this ignorant wench with the hot eyes and the
gypsy manners.

He looked into her dark eyes and glowered at her. He
backed slowly within his mind until he had a place where
he could seem to brace himself. As though he had his
shoulders against a thin hard membrane an inch in back
of his eyes.

You're too stupid.

Her hard brown hand flashed and caught him across
the mouth. She half stood up with blazing eyes and then
slowly sank back into the chair, looking a bit awed.

He found the same place within his mind to brace himself and tried this time, forcibly, yet without anger. *Nod
your head if you can understand me.*

She nodded her head violently, white teeth gleaming in
the dusky face.

Stand up and then sit down again. She obeyed like a
chastened child, demure and obedient. He found that
even that short practice enabled him to do it with more
ease.

You must learn, too. I found it by accident. He
touched his temple. *Imagine a thin hard wall in here. You
must back against it to ... be braced. And then you
must ... throw your thought from that position, thinking of each word.*

She frowned at him. She raised her eyebrows in question.

I heard nothing. Try again.

There was a black flame in the depths of her eyes. *You
are a big arrogant clown.*

I got that clearly. Try again.

She flushed. *It was anger. Anger made it easier.*

I should have told you that. How did you come here?

*A man took me to a large villa. There were other men.
I saw frightful visions. They tortured my mind. I was put
in a big gray box. It brought me here.*

Do you know why you are here?

I am aware that there are things which must be

learned. This is one of them. There will be others. This way of talking makes one weary. There is the matter of the door. It was said to us that together we could open it. Yet there is no latch.

When I snap my fingers we will both speak to the door the way we have spoken to each other, as strongly as possible, saying but one word. Open.

They both looked toward the door. He snapped his fingers. He could feel her projected thought blending with his own. The door slid slowly up out of sight into the groove overhead.

She reached the door first, ran through, and then turned and walked, docile and mild, down the corridor.

As soon as he reached the corridor, he felt the automaton will overcome his own. It turned him in the opposite direction.

A huge man who reminded him of a brown bear stepped out of a doorway to bar the hallway.

My congratulations. That was very rapid. You are a latent. Some have remained in that room for a thousand hours. Project to me. It is called para-voice.

Dake found it much harder to manage outside the room. The rigidity against which he tried to brace himself was softer, more yielding.

It was easier in the room.

"It always is. But I could receive you. We will use normal voice now. Para-voice is tiring. You will be given practice hours from time to time."

The big man took Dake's arm. Dake willed himself to pull away, but could not. He allowed himself to be led down the corridor.

"This place is called Training T. I have been here for twice your lifetime. It is work that pleases me best. Now we have our little surprise for you. The technicians found your best memory, my boy. It is ready now. You have not slept in years, you know. Not really slept. Too much conflict in your mind. Here you must sleep. Drugs are not effective. Only true sleep will heal your mind, my boy."

They came to a big door that was oddly familiar, ringing a tiny chime in the back of his weary mind.

The big brown man turned the old-fashioned knob and the door swung inward, as Dake had known it would. Dake walked into his room and the man closed the door softly behind him.

It was his room. His bed. The lamp was on over his bed. It had been a plain parchment shade, and one day he had found the silhouette of a sailing ship in a magazine. His mother had helped him cut out the hard parts. The room was in perfect scale to him. Perfect scale for an eight-year-old boy. Familiar pattern of the rag rug. The stain where he had spilled the grape juice. Place where he had crayoned the wall through the bars of the crib. No crib now. The big soft bed, with the pillows starched and white. The bed was turned down, and the flannel pajamas were laid out, where Mother always put them. Faded blue pajamas with a faint white stripe. Slippers with the heels all broken down and a lot of the lamb's wool worn off.

He undressed and put his clothes on the same chair as always and put on the pajamas and pulled the string tight at his waist and tied it. He shoved his feet into the slippers and went through the other door to the bathroom. He had to reach high to get his battered toothbrush with the chipped pink handle. The big tub had feet like white claws that clasped white porcelain spheres. Those tub feet had always fascinated him. He scrubbed his knuckles because there probably wouldn't be much time in the morning before school. The mirror was too high. He couldn't see his face unless he pulled the stool over and stood on it. But he was too sleepy for the interesting game of making horrid faces at yourself. The worst one was when you put your fingers in the corners of your mouth and pulled.

He padded back into his bedroom, closing the bathroom door behind him. He looked at his books and ran his fingers over the backs of the bindings. He opened a cigar box and looked at the shells he'd collected at Marblehead last summer. He turned out the light and went over to the window and opened it. He knelt for a time with his chin on the sill and looked out. Boston lighted

the sky. He could see the familiar single streetlight across
the backyards. It was haloed with soft snow. Snow was
falling in Chelsea, sticking to the bare branches of the big
elm in the back yard.

Somebody in the neighborhood had Christmas carols
on the radio. He wondered if he'd get the bike. They said
it was too dangerous in the street, and the police wouldn't
let you ride on the sidewalk. Heck, you could be careful,
couldn't you?

He crossed the dark room, knelt for the barest mini-
mum of prayer, and scrambled up between the crisp
sheets, nestling down, pulling the blankets up over him. A
red bike. Joey's was blue.

He yawned and turned onto his side, warm and certain
in the knowledge that after he was asleep his mother
would look in, tuck the blankets in, kiss him. He could
hear Daddy down in the kitchen with some of his friends.
He heard the low voices and then the rich explosion of
baritone laughter, suddenly hushed. He guessed Mother
was telling them not to make so much noise.

He banged at the pillow, turned onto his other side,
and gently coasted down the long velvet slope on the
magical red bike, into the deep sweet shadows of sleep.

He came vaguely awake when she came in, and he
stirred at the touch of her lips. "You think I'll get it?"

"Get what, dear?"

Irritation at such density. "The bike. The red bike."

"We'll have to wait and see, won't we? Now go to
sleep, dear."

Firm hand fixing the blankets. He was faintly aware of
the tallness of her standing over him, the faint sweet scent
of her. The floor creaked as she crossed to the window,
closed it a little. Somewhere people were laughing in the
night. She closed his door behind her as she left the
room. She hummed to herself as she headed toward the
stairs.

CHAPTER ELEVEN

School was getting harder all the time. That darn Miss Crowe. Always making it tough just before vacation. All the kids were excited about the Chinese invading Korea. He wished he'd been a Marine in Korea. Patrols. Fire fights.

That darn Miss Crowe. "Children, we are going to study projection." She wrote it on the board, spelling it as she wrote. "Now you all know what electricity is." She stepped to the front seats and tapped Joey on the head. She made that funny smile, like when she thinks her jokes are funny, and said, "Joseph's head is full of electricity. It's what he thinks with." The whole class laughed and Joey got red as a beet.

"But Joseph's electrical field is unorganized. Think of one of those big signs overlooking the Common. Now those signs spell out words. All the light bulbs light at once to spell out a word. If all those little light bulbs were flickering, going on and off without any order at all, we couldn't read the word, could we? Sometimes Joseph, by accident, makes all the little bulbs light at once, usually when he's very excited or upset, and then we can sometimes see his thoughts, not clearly of course, but enough to know for a split second what he is thinking. It happens so seldom, however, that we never recognize it as true projection. We call it a hunch, or a good guess. In projection we will all learn first how to make the words clear. And after we have made the words clear, then we will learn how to project real images. We'll project dogs and cats and new toys and everything we can imagine."

"A red bike?" Dake said without thinking.

Miss Crowe looked at him. "Yes, a red bike, Dake. But I shouldn't advise you to try and ride it." Everybody laughed at him and he got as red as Joey had been.

Maralyn, who was always asking questions and bringing junk to Miss Crowe, stuck her hand up.

"Yes, dear?"

"Miss Crowe, if all that goes on in somebody's head, how can somebody else see it?"

"It isn't exactly seeing, Maralyn. Joseph has energy in his brain. Projection is a case of learning to focus that energy. And because each of us uses the same sort of energy to do our thinking, Joseph can learn to focus it so strongly that he actually does our thinking for us."

"Suppose I don't want *him* doing my thinking for *me*," Maralyn said with contempt.

"As we are learning projection, dear, we will also learn how to close our minds against it."

Maralyn sat down, flouncing a little in the seat. Dake hated her.

Miss Crowe went back to her desk. Joey looked happy to have her stop tapping his head. It seemed to make him nervous.

"Now, class, this will be a little demonstration to show you what we will be able to do, every one of us, before summer vacation."

Dake liked that part. She just sat there looking at the class, and, gosh, she put songs in your head, and band music, and she made some poems, and then a whole lot of puppies came running in through the closed doors, and bright-colored birds flew around and made a heck of a racket. It was really keen the way she could do that.

But after that first day, the fun was all gone. It got dull and hard. Standing up there like a goof and trying to give the whole class some dopey word. Miss Crowe would write it on a piece of paper, write a lot of things on pieces of paper and you drew out your piece and it was always some dopey word. House, farm, cow, seashell, road, lamp, doctor. Never good words like bike, pirate, sloop, robber, pistol.

You had to practice at home, too, and Mother and

Daddy could do it so much easier and better than you could that you felt like you'd never learn anything. He guessed it was important stuff, all right. Miss Crowe had cut out all the other subjects, and it was nothing but that projection, projection, all day long. She kept saying you had to learn it when your mind was young, or something.

Christmas came, and no red bike because it was too dangerous. There were skis, but it turned warm and there wasn't any snow. He horsed around with Joey most of the vacation and they projected stuff at each other, and he worked at trying to make a bike he could see, even if he couldn't ride it, like Miss Crowe said.

He got so he could make some stuff, but not a good bike. One afternoon he made a real sharp red bike, right in his room, but he couldn't hold on to it. It got shimmery and went away and he couldn't bring it back.

When school started again the whole class got so they could do the words loud and clear. Then there were little sentences. Kid stuff. I see the horse. The horse sees me. My uncle owns a cat. It has kittens. It sleeps in the barn. That Maralyn was a pain. She projected words so sharp they hurt your head and you wished there was some way you could put your fingers in your ears to stop the racket.

Next they got hard words. You want to do *cat* and you can think of a cat all right, but a word like *thought* or *religion* or *doubt*—it was tough to think of ways to put it across. But finally they all got that. And then they had to take turns going further and further down the hall and doing the hard sentences. Maralyn was the only one who could go way out in the school yard by the swings and still make you hear. It was pretty faint and you had to strain for it, but she could do it.

Next came learning how to shut it out. In order to push out the words you had to sort of brace yourself against a sort of imaginary membrane in your mind. Miss Crowe called that the "first screen." Finally they all got the trick of being able to sort of get that membrane around in front of your thoughts. You had to kind of slide through it and then hold it up in the way, and it blocked out all the projection. It sure was a relief to be able to stop hearing that screamy noise Maralyn could put in your head.

Miss Crowe said that because her mind was stronger, she could project right through your screen if she really poured on the coal, but that would hurt you and the screen would have to heal up before you could project or receive or anything. She said that she had four screens she could put up, one behind the other. She said that with all of them down, she could catch projections even when the person wasn't trying to project, provided they didn't have any screen up. She said that when they had all learned how to project and receive selectively, and could make images, and knew how to use the second screen, then they could all be called Stage One. To get to be a Stage Two like her and use all screens you had to really work at it. Gee, it looked as if school would last the rest of his life.

But it got to be sort of fun when they got so they could make the images. Illusions, Miss Crowe sometimes called them. It turned out Joey was better at it than Maralyn, and that sure scalded Maralyn. Joey had an animal book home, and one day he about startled Miss Crowe out of her wits by having a giant sloth hanging from the transom over the door to the classroom. Dake worked on the red bike until he could make it with no trouble. After a while it got dull, making the bike, so he made other things. But working on the bike had helped. He could make things almost as good as Joey could. Joey got in bad trouble, though, with Miss Crowe. He got his hands on a medical book with illustrations, and he kept making little tiny naked women running around when Miss Crowe wasn't looking, and Maralyn told on him. Miss Crowe said if he kept acting up, she'd burst his first screen and give him a long rest until he learned how to use his new skill. Her nose always got white when she got mad.

Dake made a great big dog that followed him around and only disappeared when he forgot it. Once in his room he made a boy that looked just like him, exactly, and that scared him a little. But it gave him new ideas. Once on the way home with Joey, he saw Maralyn and so he made a duplicate of her standing right in front of her, only Maralyn had her head under her arm. Maralyn went screaming into her house and told Miss Crowe the next day, and he got the word, just as Joey had. Then she gave the whole class a big dull lecture about misusing your talents and all that sort of thing. He and Joey could talk easy to each other in that para-voice, but it was funny how it seemed quieter and nicer to really talk, and say the words.

The big test came right before summer vacation, and each one of them had to go all alone up to the principal's office. A lot of funny-looking people were sitting around. Dake was pretty nervous. He had to talk in para-voice to each one of them separately, and then to the whole group and then to any two of them. Then he was told to screen himself and they pushed at the screen. They pushed so hard it hurt badly, but he didn't yell, and they didn't break the screen. He guessed they were just testing to see how strong it was. He had the feeling they could bust through in a minute if they wanted to. Next they made him lift the first screen and they pushed on the second one. He wasn't so sure of how to use the second one, and it was a different kind of pain, not quite as sharp, but worse somehow. Then he had to illusion up a bunch of stuff. From a list. It was pretty hard stuff. A little full moon the size of an apple, and a life-size army jeep, and his father and mother. They gave him a chance to fix up the illusions a little when they didn't look quite right. The jeep was the worst, because he couldn't remember how the front end was supposed to look, so it stayed a little bit misty until he put a Chevy front end on it.

They told him he'd passed and the big brown-looking man shook hands with him and he walked out to go back to the class. But he walked out into a long shining black corridor that he'd never seen before.

There was a funny twisty feeling in his brain and suddenly he remembered where he was. The room, the shell collection, the red bike he didn't get. They were all twenty-six long years ago. Joey had been dead for years. Maralyn had married Vic Hudson and gone to live in

Australia. He desperately resented being drawn back up into life, out of the best years, the long golden endless years.

The big brown man took his arm.

"You did as well as I expected you to, Dake."

"Was it all . . ."

"Illusion? Of course. We find that if we regress the student to the happiest time of his life, before the world began to disappoint him, it increases his speed of receptivity. You've spent a great many weeks meeting each day with one of our better instructors and illusionists."

Dake felt as though the illusion of the lost years had somehow healed him, made him stronger and more certain.

"And now I have the abilities of a Stage One?"

"Just the mental abilities. There are some physical skills to learn."

"It seems to me like a crazy contradiction. You teach me something that, if you taught it to . . . everyone on earth, all the bad things would be erased. Hate, fear. No more conflict."

The man continued to walk him down the featureless corridor. "Quite true," he said mildly.

"Why isn't this knowledge used for good?"

"This answer may seem very indirect to you. But it is an answer. I am a failure. Too mild. Too sympathetic. I bleed from the heart too often, Dake. So I'm better off here."

"Indirect? It doesn't mean anything."

"Don't be impatient. You've graduated to one of the huts near the game fields. We've seen the last of you here . . . until next time."

"Where do I go?"

"Just go out that door. The instruction beam will pick you up. You'll find that you'll walk to exactly where you are supposed to go."

Dake walked across a field of spongy aqua-colored grass. He turned and looked back, saw the low black buildings, the grotesquely enormous trees, the metallic plain beyond with its intensely orderly arrangement of cubes. The brown man stood in the black doorway.

Good luck!

Dake lifted an arm, turned and went on, feeling only a complete certainty that he was headed in the right direction.

The huts ringed the enormous game fields. They were of the same featureless black of the larger buildings so far away that the big trees over them were on the far horizon. The huts were set far apart. There was a single communal building. The guiding influence led him directly to the communal building. On the far side of the game fields was a small group, too far away for him to see what they were doing. There were more of the violet-eyed non-human clerks in the communal building. They had a grotesque and peculiar grace of their own. The influence over him was not as strong as when he had first reported. His acceptance was not as automatic. And their attitude was different. They seemed servile, humble, overcourteous as several small objects were handed to him.

If it would please you, these objects should be taken to your hut. We cannot approach the huts or we would take them.

Which hut?

They all made thin sounds of pain, cringing before him.

Too strong, too strong. The words were sweet-singing in his brain. One of them moved carefully around him to the door, pointed. *That one, Earthling. Then you must join the others.*

He crossed to the hut, carrying the odd objects in his hands. The interior was stark. Bed, table, chair. He placed the objects on the table, fingered them curiously, joined the group at the far side of the game fields.

He counted them as he approached. Eleven. Some turned and looked toward him. He stopped abruptly as a stone-faced middle-aged woman appeared directly in front of him. Her expression was wise, sardonic, half-amused.

"Lorin, I see. Consider yourself a straggler. No one

seems to organize things properly anymore. Where is the
Gypsy girl?"

"I haven't any idea."

"Meet your fellow sufferers."

She gave the names quickly as Dake faced the group.
His glance moved across one lean tough masculine face,
moved quickly back to it. "Tommy! Good Lord, I . . ."
He took two steps toward the familiar man and then
stopped suddenly, wary. He glanced toward the stone-
faced woman who had called herself Marina.

"No, I'm not an illusion," Tommy said in his slow familiar drawl. He approached Dake, gripped his hand
strongly. "Satisfy you?"

Marina said, "You may take a break, Watkins. Go off
and gabble with your long-lost Dake Lorin."

They walked apart from the others. Dake covered his
confusion by saying, "How long? Not since the war, is it?
Last I heard you left the city desk and went to Florida to
run some jerkwater newspaper, Tommy. I envied you. It
seemed to be a good answer."

Are you thinking I have any answers to . . . all this?

Dake stared at him. *I was hoping as much.*

*And I'm hoping you have some answers. I don't know
where we are, how we got here, or whether you happen
to be a figment of my diseased imagination.*

Tommy dropped to the springy odd-colored grass and
spoke aloud. "Nobody else in the . . . ah . . . class has
the vaguest idea. See, we've got a couple of Chinese, and
a Malay, and a pair of Austrians. But no language problems, chum, in para-voice. Sentence construction comes
through a little strange sometimes. We do a lot of chatting. So I can tell you just what happened to you, Dake.
You got mixed up in something-or-other, and so many
weird things were beginning to happen you thought you
were going off your rocker. So finally you found yourself
in New York or Madrid where they slapped you in a gray
box and you tumbled out here, and these characters
began to teach you stuff that's patently impossible. Oh, we
have long discussions. Many of them about reality. Big
question. Are we really here?"

Dake sat near him. "How did you get here?"

"Started to do a series on a guy doing some fantastic work in agriculture. I began to get the weird idea somebody was guiding him. Steering his mind for him. Clues led to a racketeer named Miguel Larner in New York. Went to see Larner. He nearly drove me crazy. Almost, but not quite. So here I am."

"Mine is about the same. I'll tell you about it later. Right now, Tommy, what do we know? Somehow we got onto a different planet. We've run into a culture and a technology far superior to ours. They're training us to raise hell on earth."

"I go along with that, Dake. On the surface, an evil pitch. Underneath, I . . . don't know. There is something . . . terribly important that we don't know yet. When we know it, it will somehow explain everything. Ever dream you have discovered the ultimate answer to everything and wake up with it just on the edge of your mind?"

"What goes on here, at this place?"

"You get your hut and they organize your day like it was a YMCA summer camp. Do this, do that. A few physical skills. And mostly mental skills. They stretch hell out of your brain. Memory, analysis, and so on. Things come back in a funny way. I can replay from memory every chess game I ever played and every bridge hand I ever held. A year ago that would have been a crazy thought. Right now we're struggling with something called a Pack B."

"What's that?"

"Something you'll have to experience for yourself, baby. Another thing. Have you ever had such an almost overpowering feeling of physical well-being?"

"I hadn't thought of it. I . . . guess not."

"Has air ever smelled as good, or food tasted as good? Every day seems like Saturday."

"You sound happy here. What have you done, Tommy? Found a home?"

Tommy gave him a bland look. "Maybe. I'm waiting for the great revelation. We all are." He stood up, looked soberly down at Dake for a moment. "Here is one clue to think over. We see quite a few people around who never came off earth. They're all manlike. Just funny variations here and there. All in the same general form, however. And, Dake, listen. Every single one of them treats us as though we were all little tin Jesuses. Come on. Join the group. Marina's ready to howl."

They rejoined the group. Marina formed them into a hollow circle. Practice in cooperative illusion, she said. Marina created the illusion—an exceptionally lovely girl who strolled around and around inside the formal circle. At any moment, just as the girl walked in front of you, Marina might cancel the illusion. It was up to the nearest student to re-create her so quickly and perfectly that there was barely any hiatus of nothingness. Dake was clumsy the first time. He saw that it had to be done in such a way that the stride was unbroken. The second time it happened directly in front of him he did better. A second girl joined the first and they walked hand in hand. And then a third. Marina made their costumes more intricate. She made them walk faster. It became an exhausting exercise in hair-trigger reflexes, in memorization and visualization of all details. After over an hour of it, Dake felt as though his head would burst.

There was food, and rest, and another session. Mass illusion this time. Create as many people as you can, to the outermost limitations of your resources, bearing in mind constantly that each individual thus created had to be remembered and concentrated on *in toto* or the illusion would become evanescent. At first Dake could handle no more than six. By the end of the session he had more than doubled it, and was rewarded with Marina's sour smile.

There were variations on those games day after day. At night the alien stars would pinpoint the sky with brightness. He spent the rare leisure hours with his friend, Watkins. They guessed and pondered and found no rational answer.

Apprehensive beings were brought to the game fields. They were not quite human when examined closely. They did not seem so much frightened as awed. And, using them as subjects, Marina taught the class the fundamentals of control. It required a more massive concentration of energy than para-voice, or illusioning, and it was most difficult to give proper neural directions. Even Marina could cause only an approximation of a normal walk, and balance was difficult to maintain. The controlled beings often fell onto the soft turf. Range was slowly increased, and when the class was adept, they were permitted to practice control on each other, being careful always to take both screens out of the way before accepting control. Dake found that he did not like the feeling of psychic nakedness that came when neither of his two mental screens protected him. After he had run Tommy awkwardly into the side of a hut when trying to control him through the door, Tommy had rubbed his bruised nose and said, "As a superman, kid, you're a waste of time."

It gave them a new description of their abilities. The supermen. The endowed ones. The little gods who would, they hoped, walk the earth. The best daydreams were about what could be done with the new abilities.

Tommy said, "Nobody has ever been able to get my brother-in-law off the bottle. I'm going to give that boy such a roomful of snakes and little pink elephants that he'll gag whenever he sees a liquor advertisement."

Dake said, "I'm going to control every Pak-Indian I meet. Make them drop to their knees before the Great Lorin."

"Seriously, Dake, what are we going to do with all these . . . talents?"

"We don't have to earn a living. Just control the cashier and have him hand you the money. Or give him an illusion of a few thousand rupees for deposit. He'll mark the book and when you walk out of the bank it will disappear out of the drawer."

"You have larceny in your heart."

"Tommy, I keep remembering a brown-haired girl named Karen Voss. I know now that she was trained here. Most of the things she bewildered me with, I think I could do. But she helped me get out of a bad spot, and somebody stronger than she has ripped her screens."

"Gives me a headache to think about it."

"Think a minute. Was the person who damaged her trained somewhere else? Are there two groups raising hell with each other? Is earth a battlefield? If so, we're just a couple of likely recruits."

"I'm not fighting anyone else's war," Tommy said firmly. "I had a dandy of my own once."

The next day, control was dropped and instruction in the Pack B's began again. Dake quickly learned the sequence of the control wheels and how to use them. Visualization was something else again. A hundred times he tried. A hundred times he tried to cover a distance of ten feet, and each time felt the sickening sensation of negative mass, and each time achieved plus mass in the exact place where he had started. Marina explained that the visualization of the intended destination had to be far stronger than the visualization required for illusioning. He would memorize each blade of grass, each irregularity of the earth, step back and try again. Tommy suddenly learned how. He was ecstatic with this new sense of freedom. He was obnoxiously ecstatic. He flicked about, endlessly, pausing only to wave derisively toward where Dake stood and struggled.

Dake tried again and again and again. And another failure. He was about to try again when he suddenly realized that he had covered the distance. He backed up and tried again. Slowly he discovered that the strength of the visualization was actually more important than the exactness of it. He set off after Tommy, slowly improving his skill.

For days the class played a mad game of tag around the huge game fields. Then they were taken into open country and permitted to use the full range of the Pack B. There were races across empty miles of landscape where the high trees formed the only reference points. They learned that you could visualize the face of a friend as though it were a yard in front of you, and then make the shift. If the friend was within range of your Pack B, you would suddenly appear in front of him. The sequence of days was confused. New skills, new abilities, and something else, too. A group pride.

In one of her rare informative moods Marina said, "Selection has to be a trial by fire. If you can be broken, you will break. None of you did. And thus we can be assured that you will not break in quite another way—that you will not begin to think that these new powers set you apart from mankind, that you will not misuse them for personal gain. We are called Earthling. It is a good title."

There was a day of pageant, of intense competition. The illusions were watched by vast crowds, who made sighing sounds of approval.

After the crowds had gone, Marina said, "There is nothing more I can teach you. There is only one last thing for you to learn. Those who are already on tour must instruct you in that. We will see you here twice again before you are . . . ready."

They went back to the long low black buildings of first instruction. They did not plod across the fields in the gray dusk. They flicked across the flat plains, appearing, disappearing, appearing further on. They projected to each other, writing the questioning words bright in each other's minds.

They were given rooms. In the middle of the night Dake was awakened. The clothes he had arrived in were waiting. He dressed on command, and was taken to the place of the cubes. Hard pain struck him. He clambered through the orifice into the rock cavern. He walked up the slanting glow of the tunnel and into Miguel Larner's dioramic garden. It was late afternoon. Karen sat alone, and she smiled at him.

He went to her quickly. He tried to project to her, to ask her if she was well. He felt the projected thought strike screens rigidly drawn, rebound as though from metal. The rebuff angered him.

"I suppose I report to Miguel," he said.

"He's gone, Dake. It was a very impressive funeral."

"Dead!"

"An illusion was buried. Miguel has . . . gone. He finished what he had to do. Martin Merman is in charge."

"Do I report to him?"

"He's not here. What gives you the idea you have to report to anybody?"

"I thought . . ."

"Go to the same room you were in before. Stay there until called."

CHAPTER TWELVE

Dake went to the room. He found clothes that would fit him. He set the diorama on automatic control to give him an approximation of day and night. Food was brought at regular intervals. There was a projector, micro-books, music. He exercised to keep himself fit.

Stay there until called.

He had detected a warmth, a friendliness in her before. It had disappeared. He felt put-upon, neglected. And he was indignant.

At times he would drop both screens and listen, almost trembling with the effort to be receptive. He would get merely the vague awareness of others somewhere near him. No thoughts ever came through.

One evening she tapped lightly at the door, came in, unasked, and sat down.

"Are you getting impatient?"

"I'm bored."

"The other night you made a detailed illusion of me, and had me sit and talk nicely to you for a time. I'm flattered, Dake."

"I didn't know I'd be spied on here."

"We're all very interested in you. We're interested in all fresh new dewy-eyed Stage Ones."

"You've changed, Karen."

"Karen Voss? That was a hypno-fix. A nice cover story. You can call me Karen if it will make you feel more at ease."

"Thank you," he said with grave dignity.

She laughed at him and he flushed. He said, "I learned

enough to know that you made a considerable sacrifice
for me."

Her eyes changed for a moment. She made a vague
gesture. "It is everyone's duty to recruit. Material is
scarce, you know. It always has been. You were my little
gesture, so Merman has made me your house mother.
Rather unfair, I think. Stage Ones are dull."

"I had an old friend. I met him at Training T. He kept
talking about an ultimate answer. Does giving any ultimate answer come under the heading of responsibilities of
the house mother?"

"It helped you, Dake. You're not quite as stuffy."

"I'm getting damn sick of mystery."

"We'll take a walk. Come on. See the great world outside. Now see if you can remember the lobby well enough
to shift to it. Wait a moment. I'll check with Johnny to
see if we have any strangers around." She paused a moment. "It's all right."

He made the lobby as quickly as he could. Yet she was
there ahead of him, smiling at him.

"See what we have, Johnny?" she said, taking Dake's
arm.

"In spite of all wagers to the contrary," Johnny said.
Welcome home.

Thanks.

"I sometimes think you Ones are the worst snobs of
all," Karen said. "I'll have to orient you, Dake. A June
evening. 1978. That article you published last year made
quite a stir. Don't walk so fast! But you repudiated it. So
all the excitement died down, and people forgot about it
in the excitement of George Fahdi's assassination. You
were convicted of a Disservice and sentenced to ten years
of hard labor. The lovely Patrice was in a nursing home
and couldn't bribe you out of it. A poor little Stage One
had a hideous time keeping the illusion of you going
through the quick trial, sentence and shipment. As soon
as you were in the labor camp, he quit, of course, so now
you're a fugitive from justice. But they aren't going to
hunt too hard. Martin bribed the right people."

"You're going too quickly, Karen. I don't . . ."

"Don't try. We'll just have a little stroll."

He held his screens firm, so that there was no possibility of her catching any fragment of his plan. He casually slipped his hand into his pocket, built up a powerful visualization of the hotel room where he had last stayed in New York. He worked the small wheels with his thumbnail. The shift to the hotel room was instantaneous. A puffy white-haired man in a dressing gown gaped at him. "How did you get in here, sir?" A pretty vacant-eyed girl wearing very little of anything came to the bathroom door and stared at him.

"Wrong room," Dake said. "Sorry."

"Couldn't you knock, dammit?"

"Sorry," Dake said. He moved to the door, unlocked it, hurried out into the corridor.

He went down the hallway, conscious of his conspicuous height. He went down the stairs and out into the warm June evening. He was painfully aware of how the months of Training T had heightened all his perceptions. Sounds seemed too loud, impressions too vivid. The world was a swarming mass of lurid, confusing detail. He had to get away from it, get away to some quiet place where he could think and plan.

He went to another hotel, gave illusion money to the clerk, pocketed his real change, tipped the bellhop with some of it. The room was small, depressingly dingy. He turned off the lights, put a chair over by the window and sat in it, looking out at the skyline.

Funny how this was supposed to be home, yet he felt a strangeness here. As though he were no longer a part of it. He remembered his original resolve, that resolve that had never weakened—learn everything you can and come home and use it to expose them. Let the guy in the street know that he was being pushed around.

And the men in the street would ask WHY?

Dake did not know why. The thing seemed planless. Another extension of the games field.

Now be coherent with yourself. Collate the data. Set up an operating plan. Through the use of illusion you could land a space ship in New Times Square, march a goggle-headed crew of Martians down Broadway. That, perhaps, would start men thinking about interference—on an extra-terrestrial basis.

"You're a hard man to find," Karen said, behind him.

He turned quickly, almost relieved at momentarily escaping the necessity of making a plan.

She said, "That illusion with the money did it. I caught the direction of that. You can't use anything you've learned, Dake, without it being detectable."

The meager light of the night city touched her face, her cool alien eyes. She looked at him with that remote speculation of an entomologist awaiting an emergence from the cocoon.

He tried to project, to probe her mind. The screen was like metallic rock.

"All your tricks," he said, almost incoherently. "All your dirty little inhuman devices. They——"

"All *our* tricks, Dake."

"Not mine. I didn't ask for it. I went along with it. No choice at all." He stood up, towering over her, his back to the light. "Now the tricks make me ashamed. They make me a . . . mutation. They destroy the meaning of being a man."

"How noble!"

"You can't trace me if I don't use them, can you?"

"Can a man will himself to stop using his arms?"

He half turned from her to conceal the hand he slipped into his pocket. He thought of a ruse. Phone booths have a cookie-cutter similarity. He visualized quickly, flipping the wheels, feeling the surge of sickening nothingness, the sudden recapitulation of himself staring at the black phone a foot from his eyes. He stepped out of the booth, saw that he was in the hotel lobby downstairs, that the Pack B had selected the most immediate target visualization.

He walked out onto the street. Just as he tried to lose himself in the crowd, the thought arrowed faintly into his mind. *Dake! Run and we will kill you. We will have to. If you can hear me, come back.*

His stride faltered for a moment, and then he moved

on to lose himself in the crowd. He instinctively hunched his shoulders, walked with knees slightly bent to reduce his towering height.

Learn what they can give you and use it against them. He had spent his life fighting. The equation was clear. The logic was impeccable. If *they* had the abilities he had learned, then they could put an end to the conflict on earth. They did not. Thus they were unfriendly to mankind. And man would have to know and learn. Man would have to recognize the enemy within the gates.

He remembered the one who had injured Karen, injured that previous, more understandable Karen. They seemed to fight among themselves, but with grotesquely gallant little rules. So Earth was an extension of the games field. A place where you could be aware of your own superiority. Make the silly little creatures jump. They had made him jump, had killed Branson, had driven Patrice mad. They were like cruel children let loose in a zoo with loaded rifles.

A slow-moving prowl car slid a spotlight beam across him, went on. He could hear the metallic chatter of its radio. There would be danger from two sources. According to Karen, Martin Merman had arranged it so that the authorities would not be too eager to recapture him after his supposed escape. Merman could easily reverse that. His great height made him feel naked on the streets. He knew that through his newly acquired talent of control, of illusioning, or para-voice, he could make any attempt to take him a heartbreaking matter to any federal officer. But his escape attempts would, as Karen had told him, enable them to find him easily. As long as he used none of his new abilities, they could only recognize him visually, and confirm it by projecting against the first screen in his mind.

The faces of the people on the night streets depressed him. The months on Training T seemed to have given him a heightened susceptibility to mood. He could feel the waves of tension, and despair, and aimless discontent. Cold taffy faces and metronome eyes and life-broken mouths. An animal walking the city, with the tired inviting flex and clench of buttocks, with soupy opacity of eye. He walked through futility, drowning in it. And then, slowly, began to see other things. Small things. A young boy with a rapt, dedicated face, eyes of a stricken angel, looking upward at one of the pre-war buildings, at the simple perfect beauty of structural integrity. A couple, hand in hand, who would have been alone on the busiest street in the world. An old man shuffling along—the light slanting against a face that had been twisted and torn and broken by life, leaving nothing but a look of calm and peace, a look in which there was that beauty which is sometimes the by-product of torture. Pride made his eyes smart. Try to smash them utterly, and there was always something left in the ruins. Something priceless, eternal.

As he walked, wondering where he should hide, he remembered a column in a lighter vein that he had done long ago, in, it seemed, someone else's lifetime. Dr. Oliver Krindle, psychiatrist, whose hobby was psychic research. He remembered Krindle as one of those rare, warm men not damaged by too much knowledge of the human soul. The column had been about Krindle's endless and skeptical effort to track down psychic phenomena, about the two incidents out of all those years which Krindle felt did not lend themselves to any satisfactory explanation—except the obvious one that the persons reporting them lied.

He looked up Krindle's address in a phone book, walked fifteen blocks to the narrow lightless street. He had remembered that Krindle lived alone over his office. He remembered the good and ancient brandy Krindle had served, making a ceremony of the little ritual. Brandy in a room lined with books—as though Krindle had found some special way to preserve the good things in a world in which good things were no longer understood.

There was a dim light in the hallway. He pressed the button, heard a distant ringing. Across the street, shirt-sleeved men and weary women sat on front steps, their voices slow in the warm night, their laughter oddly dreary.

Dr. Oliver Krindle came down the stairs. Dake saw the

thick naked ankles, the worn slippers, the battered robe, the deceptive face of a shaven Santa. Krindle turned on the light over the door and peered through, then made a great rattling of chains and bolts.

"Come in, Lorin. Come in! Damn careful these days. Hoodlums, cretins. Violence for its own sake. That's the kind that frightens you. For profit, that is understandable. Too many people like to look at blood. Maybe it's always been that way. Come on up. I've been listening to music. Choral stuff tonight. Lots of voices in my room, eh?"

Dake followed the man up the stairs, to the quiet room he remembered. Dr. Krindle waved him to a chair, said, "I'll start this one again from the beginning. No one is in too much of a hurry for this, Lorin." He turned on the player again.

Dake leaned back in the chair, let the music sweep over him like a vast warm tide. Krindle moved slowly, making two drinks, setting one down at Dake's elbow. The music was a rich sanity, a reaffirmation of faith in man, a denial of the things he had learned.

The music stopped and Krindle turned it off. They sat in the silence for a time. Ice tinkled in Dake's glass as he raised it to his lips.

"I have read about you, Lorin. You've been busy. Disservice, sentence, escape. I knew you would be a fugitive someday. I did not know when or how."

"But you knew why?"

"Of course. You meet environment in too direct a manner. So your environment is embarrassed. It doesn't like defects pointed out. So it destroys you."

"Martyr?"

"Yes. Without purpose. Your defeat does not add impetus to any creed or group or movement. The solitary man. The flaw, possibly, is in believing too much in yourself. If that is a flaw. I don't know. Once upon a time I told myself I would never compromise. Oh, I was young and brave. Now I look back on life. A life of listening to the anxious daydreams of neurotic women. Little minds so shallow that they present but one surface, Lorin."

"What is normalcy, Oliver? Stability?"

"It doesn't exist. Just a convenient line you draw. Everybody overlaps that line at some point, and deviates widely at another. Add up all the aspects of an individual, and you can only classify him as an individual. No two men have ever been mentally sick or mentally well in the same way—with the exception of physiological mental illness. We are all, unfortunately, unique. How simple my profession would be if I could type people, safely and accurately!"

"Suppose it were your function to drive a man mad. How would you go about it?"

"First I would change your terminology. How would I go about creating a mental illness? The classic way is to present him with an insoluble problem, and make it necessary for survival for him to solve that problem. The rat in a maze with no exit."

"Suppose you could make his senses give him . . . nonsense messages."

"Wouldn't that be another aspect of the same classic problem, Dake Lorin? To survive, it is necessary to be able to trust what your eyes and ears and touch and smell tell you. If the data they present to the brain are patently impossible, then the subject has a classic problem. I must trust my senses in order to survive. My senses cannot be trusted. What do I do? But aren't you thinking of a result rather than a cause. A patient will hallucinate when he can no longer stand the sane messages his senses give him. A wife is unfaithful. So he hears a voice coming out of the fireplace. It says to kill her."

"What happens if the cart is before the horse?"

"Will he kill her, you mean? That depends on how dependent he is on his ears and eyes and sense of touch. Roughly, I would say the more meager the intelligence, the more likely the patient is to obey a false message. What have your false messages been?"

Dake studied his thick hard knuckles. "I looked into a mirror. The left side of my face was a naked skull. I touched it. It was hard and cold. Two persons with me saw it, too. One went mad and one fainted."

"I would say that you had subconsciously recognized the duality of your life, recognized a death wish."

"If two others saw it?"

"Once I had a patient who resented the way people on the street would stop and pet his three-headed purple dog. It followed him everywhere."

"Suppose I told you, Oliver, that I can make you stand up against your will, pick up that record off the turntable and break it on the hearth."

"Perhaps you could, if I were willing to submit to hypnosis."

"Suppose I tell you that I can create a . . . three-headed purple dog right here and that you will be able to see it. Or tell you that I can project words into your mind, so that you can know what I am saying without my speaking."

Oliver Krindle took a slow sip of his drink. "I would say that you have had much strain lately. You were trying to help the world. The world destroyed your effectiveness. You cannot admit that you are ineffective. The struggle is too important to you. You compensate by endowing yourself with strange psychic gifts which seem to restore your effectiveness."

"Why have you always been interested in psychic research?"

"For the same reason that a man who is trying to grow an orchard will be interested in a thick dark woods next door."

"Then you believe, Oliver, that there is much that you do not know."

"Do I look that arrogant? Of course there is much I do not know."

"Have you ever wondered if all the mystery in our world might come from one special source?"

"God, Martians, Irish visions?"

"What if the world we know is a test tube? A culture dish? A continuous bacterial conflict?"

Oliver half closed his eyes. "Interesting from a speculative point of view. But it has been done too many times before. Show me the agency."

"I'm one of them."

Oliver opened his eyes wide. "It would please me, Dake Lorin, if you would stay here tonight."

"I'm one of them, but I don't want to be one of them. They're after me. They'll kill me, and mankind will never know what . . . opposes it. I can't demonstrate talents, because they are sensitive to that. They can find me."

"Lorin, I . . ."

Dake leaned forward. "Shut up a minute. I'm going to take a chance. But I am going to make it very quick. You'll have to get whatever you can get from it in a very few seconds."

"Have you thought what you would do if your . . . mysterious powers fail?"

"That's why I came here. If they fail, I've been mad for months on end. But they won't fail. Do you see that corner of the table, directly under the lamp. There is nothing there, Oliver, is there?"

"Of course not, but . . ."

"And you are resisting any attempt at hypnosis, are you not?"

"Yes, but . . ."

"Watch the corner of the table," Dake said softly. He did the simplest illusion he could think of. A featureless white cube, about three inches on a side. He let it remain there on the corner of the table for no longer than two seconds, and then erased it utterly.

He had watched the cube. He turned his eyes to Oliver Krindle's face. Under the cheerful red cheeks the flesh tone had gone chalky gray. The glass trembled violently as he lifted it to his lips. Some of the drink sloshed out onto the ancient dressing gown. The glass chattered as he set it back down on the broad arm of his chair.

"I may not have much time, Oliver. They may come for me. I want you to know . . ."

"One of the most startling demonstrations of hypnosis," Krindle said, too loudly, "that I have ever seen."

"I came to you because of all the men I know, you are the most likely to react to this in a sane and competent manner."

Krindle chuckled, too loudly, artificially. "Sometimes the sick mind can perform startling things, Lorin. Think of the cataleptic trance, for example. Think of the classic sign of the stigmata, induced through auto-hypnosis. You startled me for a moment, but I can readily understand that it is nothing but the manifestation of . . ."

Dake felt a faint warning touch against his mind. He stood up quickly. "There's no time left now, Oliver. Watch my lips." *I do not speak but you can hear my words.*

His fingertips worked the tiny wheels quickly. As the moment of nothingness weakened him, he saw Oliver still sitting there, eyes bulging glassily. The phone booth was dark. He stepped quickly out into the dark tiled corridor of a locked office building. A car rumbled by outside. He stood, holding his breath, waiting for some faint touch of awareness against his mind. There was nothing. He went up the dark metal treads of the stairs. He found a doctor's office. The door was locked. He chinned himself on the top of the frame, looked through the transom. The room was faintly lighted by the reflection of the city against the night sky. He visualized the interior and then, barely in time, realized how this would be a mistake. He broke the door lock, stretched out on a couch in the inner office. He was exhausted, and sleep came before he could plan the next day.

CHAPTER THIRTEEN

In the morning Dake left the office when the building was just coming to life. The sky was gray, the air filled with the threat of thunder. He had no money. To acquire some by extra-human means would be a grave risk. On impulse he risked turning back into the office. He found a locked tin box in the receptionist's desk. He broke it under his heel, pried the lid off, pocketed the few bills and plastic coins it contained.

There was more than enough for breakfast. He found a small grubby place, picked a morning paper off the pile by the cashier's cage.

The notice of the death of Dr. Oliver Krindle was on page three, a single paragraph. "Dr. Oliver Krindle, noted psychiatrist, phoned his intention of hanging himself to the police last night, and by the time he was cut down it was too late to revive him. The suicide note stated that his long work with the insane had at last broken his mind, and that his own prognosis was unfavorable. Police report evidence that Dr. Krindle had a visitor shortly before his death, but the identity is not known at this time."

Dake ate mechanically, not noticing the taste or texture of the food. If the sanest, soundest man he knew found it impossible to accept the disconcerting proof of inhuman deviation, to accept the knowledge of skills previously limited to legend and oddly accurate fairy stories, then who would accept it? What would a group do? Check it off to the great realm of table levitation and ectoplasmic messages from Aunt Dorrie?

He remembered one of the very ancient moving pictures to which Darwin Branson had taken him. Old pictures fascinated Darwin. He remembered the one where a tramp was given a legitimate check for one million dollars. An uncertified check. He had a fortune in his hand, and no one could accept the reality of it. Just a bum with a delusion of grandeur. In the end, he had had to tear it up, or go crazy.

And he remembered a particularly infuriating incident of his youth. One summer he had gone surf casting near Marblehead, alone on the gray dawn beach, using borrowed equipment, heaving the cut bait out as far as he could, retrieving it slowly, the surf smashing against his thighs. He was using hundred-pound test line. Suddenly a massive tug had yanked him off balance, nearly yanking the rod out of his hands. He clung desperately, thinking of the cost of replacing rod, reel and line. He had floundered in the surf and the reel had locked somehow. He wanted to brace himself and break the line, but he was yanked forward again, yanked off his feet, towed straight out with ominous speed and power. He saw at once that he would have to let the rod and reel go and swim back, or risk being drowned. Then he discovered what had locked the reel. The end of his water-soaked sweater had caught fast in the reel. He tried to rip it loose and it would not give. He had yelled in panic at the empty seascape. He was moving faster than any human could swim. The monster at the other end of the line swam steadily out, and then miraculously made a long slow turn and headed in again. It was evidently its intention to scrape the hook off on the rocks near shore. Dake at last slammed into the rocks painfully, and the line parted in that instant. He floundered to shore and sat, bleeding, panting.

It had been an exciting experience . . . until he tried to tell someone about it, experienced the blank incredulous stare, the roar of laughter. There was no proof. Nothing but wet clothes and gouged hands. You just took a tumble in the surf and thought a fish yanked on the line, boy. There's nothing in here to tow you around like that.

No one had believed him. Ever.

No one had believed in the bum with a million dollars. No one would believe in the powers he had acquired. And he could not use them and remain alive. Unless . . .

In late afternoon he found what he wanted. A twenty-five-year-old rust bucket of a War II Liberty ship, under Panama registry, which meant, of course, Brazilian control. They signed him on as a deck hand, looking only at his powerful frame, not at the lack of identification. At dusk they wallowed slowly by the shattered stub of the Statue of Liberty, heading for Jacksonville, Havana, Port au Prince, Rio. He knew that ten thousand yards was the ultimate limit of the Pack B. He knew that there had to be some limit to the space over which they could detect the psychic radiations of any extra-human application of mental force. At no time did he doubt that they would kill him if they could. It is more difficult to lie in the mind than with the lips. He wanted a chance to think. He wanted labor that would exhaust his body. He had the vague, unformed idea of taking an isolated group of people, such as the crew of the ship, and somehow forcing them to believe in what he would tell them.

The captain was a remote little man with a twitching face and two fingers missing on each hand. His name was Ryeson. The first officer ran the ship. He was a round muscular Dutchman with tangerine hair, radiation scars on his face and throat, and his name was Hagger. It was a sullen ship, a floating monument to slovenliness, dirt, unidentifiable stenches. They worked long into the night battening hatches under the incomprehensible cursings of the first officer, under the roll of the ship lights, driving wedges, lashing the canvas tight.

The next morning, cramped from the short narrow bunk, Dake was put to work by Hagger chipping paint. He and the other green hand were so elected. The other man was a professorial-looking citizen in his late thirties, with the long slow tremblings of alcoholism complicated by prono addiction. His name was Green and he had nothing to say. His reflexes were so uncoordinated that he kept hurting himself, though there was not enough strength in his blows to damage himself severely.

Dake stripped to the waist and let the June sun darken his back as he worked. As he worked monotonously he tried to organize some plan. There was one alternative. To hide for the rest of his life. Never use the new skills. Work in far places, keep quiet, let the knowledge eventually die with him. That was a remarkably unsatisfying solution. He wondered how Watkins had accepted his return to Earth. Watkins would, he guessed, conform to whatever had been asked of him, expected of him. Somewhere along the line Watkins had lost the intense need to revolt.

So lost was he in thought that he stopped working for a time, squatting on his heels, looking squinch-eyed out across the blue sea. A heavy kick in the shoulder rolled him across the greasy deck. He jumped up and faced an irate first officer.

"You take a break when I give you a break. When I don't give you a break, I want to hear that hammering."

"I'll work. But don't ever try that again, my friend."

The first officer was standing close to Dake. He glanced at the chipping hammer, shrugged and turned slowly away. He spun back, putting his weight into the spin, his meaty fist landing high on the side of Dake's face, knocking him down. As Dake tried to scramble up, the heavy kick took him in the pit of the stomach. He could see, as in a haze, the wide scarred face of the first officer grinning down at him. The foot swung back again and this time Dake, half helpless, expected that it would catch him flush in the mouth.

Dake exerted the full thrust of control, taking over the chunky body, marching it back. He pulled himself to his feet, one arm clamped across his belly, gagging for breath. The first officer's eyes had a glazed look.

"What's going on down there, mister?" the captain asked, peering down from the bridge onto the boat deck. His voice was dry, puzzled.

Dake looked up, quickly released Hagger. Hagger swayed, braced himself, made a deep grunting sound in his throat and charged directly at Dake, who had to admire his single-mindedness.

Dake caught him again, and, still angered by pain, not thinking of consequences, he set Hagger off on a blundering run toward the rail. Hard thighs hit the rail and Hagger plunged forward. As he toppled into space, Dake released control. A head, orange in the sunlight, bounced in the stern wake. A yellow life-preserver arced out from the fantail, hurled by some alert seaman who had heard the captain's surprisingly loud bellow of "Man overboard!"

They swung a boat out, manning it in a sloppy way, and recovered the first officer. He seemed remarkably chastened. Dake went back to work. He was aware that the first officer and the captain were on the bridge, talking in low tones. He could sense their eyes on him.

"Stand up, you," the captain said, startlingly close behind him. Dake stood up and turned. Captain Ryeson stood six feet away. He held a massive ancient automatic in a white steady hand, the muzzle pointing at Dake's belly. Dake was aware that the rest of the ship was disturbed. There was a clot of a dozen hands forty feet down the deck. The first officer stood just behind Ryeson and a bit to one side.

"Mister Hagger is going to knock you about a bit. I want to see what happens. He says you made him jump over the rail. Try that again and I'll blow a hole in you."

"You better forget the whole thing, Captain," Dake said quietly.

"A thing like that can bother a man. Go ahead, Mister Hagger. The whole crew is present." Hagger balled his fists, licked his lips and came tentatively in toward Dake, walking uneasily.

"Forget it, please, Captain. I won't be beaten. And I won't be . . . accountable for what I'll do to stop a beating."

"I want to know what I have aboard my ship," the captain said.

Dake was in that moment aware of the full impact of the fear and horror that normal man has for any entity that is alien. He knew that if they couldn't understand him, they would destroy him. He saw that what he should do was to cow them utterly, and quickly.

Hagger took another cautious step, his shoulders tightening. Dake's refusal to defend himself was troubling the first officer.

The captain turned quickly and jumped back away from the maraca rattle of the tail of the coiled diamondback. It struck at him and he fired. The slug screamed off the iron deck, high into the blue air. The snake was gone and the muzzle swung quickly toward Dake. He took over the captain's mind, finding it tougher than the mate's, finding it a bit harder to exert control. The mate's eyes bugged and the captain slowly put the muzzle of the gun into his mouth, closed his lips around it. The vast warted weedy head of a sea serpent shot up off the starboard bow, throwing sparkling drops into the air. It made a bass grunting noise. Dake felt quite impressed with it. The mate stood fixed in horror. Dake released the captain, who snatched the muzzle out of his mouth, once again tried to aim at Dake. Dake made him throw the automatic over the side. Dake backed until he was braced against the bulkhead. He peopled the bridge with illustrations from the books of boyhood. Blackbeard, with twists of powder that crackled and flared and stank in his beard. Long John Silver, banging the peg leg against the bridge railing. Captain Bly, with eyes like broken ice. A dead sailor, clad in conches and seaweed. For artistic balance, he added a creature of his own devising—a duplicate of Captain Ryeson who carried under each arm, like a pair of pumpkins, two grinning heads of First Officer Hagger, the tangerine hair aflame.

And he had them all lounge against the bridge rail and look down and yell with thin, hollow, obscene laughter.

Dake turned back. The mate had gone over the rail again, on the opposite side of the sea serpent. The captain stood with his eyes closed tightly. Dake heard the ripe fruit plop of seamen going over the side, dropping into the blue sea. Several tried to lower a boat, and the lines fouled, and they went over the side.

He dispersed the illusions, seeing at once that he had

gone too far. They were swimming west, away from horror, toward the faint smoky line of coast. He could control the nearest ones, but his control was not expert enough for the complicated task of swimming. Each time he would release them to avoid drowning them, they would turn like automatons and swim away from the ship. They were dwindling astern, out of his range. The captain had fallen. His face was bluish. He died as Dake was trying to revive him. Dake ran to the wheel, tried to bring the ship around. Midway in the long arc the muted thud of driving power faltered, stopped. The ship coasted, powerless. The heads had dwindled astern. He found the captain's glass and steadied it. Even as he watched, powerless to help, he saw them going under, one by one. Their initial frenzy had exhausted them. The bright head of the mate, bright against the blue sea, was the last to go. And the sea was empty. He went over the ship from end to end, carefully. A cat sat on the galley table, mincingly cleaning its paws. The engine room was empty. He and the cat shared the ship. It rolled in the ground swell, and dishes clinked. Food cooled at the long table. A wisp of smoke rose from the last fragment of a cigarette. He had overestimated their capacity to absorb horror. He dragged the captain to his cabin, tumbled him into his bunk, straightened out the dead limbs. He found the ship's safe ajar. He crammed his pockets with cash, pried fouled lines loose and managed to awkwardly lower a boat. He slid down a line and boarded it. The cranky motor started at last. He moved in numbness, in consciousness of the unpremeditated murder of twenty-one men. He thought of the one who, as he was sinking, turned and made a sign of the cross toward the devil's ship.

Blue water sparkled and danced. The boat chugged obediently toward the smear of land against the west horizon. Closer in he came on private fishing boats and gave them a wide berth. He turned south, away from an area of summer camps, away from the bright specks of colorful beach costumes, and at last found a place where he could land unobserved. The ship was out of sight, miles off the beach. This would give the world another mystery of the sea, another Marie Celeste, as inexplicable as the original. And all he had learned, through twenty-one deaths, was that it was far too easy to overestimate the capacity of man to accept horror, particularly horror that dances in the bright sunlight.

He drove the bow against coarse sand, leaped ashore and abandoned the boat, striking up across rough dunes, finding a narrow road. He turned north, walking along the shoulder, clad in the ill-fitting work clothes he had borrowed aboard the ship. Cars passed him. He found that he was near Poverty Beach, just north of Cape May. He walked to Wildwood. By mid-afternoon he was in Atlantic City. He bought clothing in a shoddy ersatz wool, waited for alterations. At nightfall he was on a crowded bus just entering the city limits of Philadelphia. Regret was a dull ache within him. If only he had been more restrained . . . perhaps it would have all been possible. A slow indoctrination of the men aboard the ship. Teach them the nature of the enemy.

But if Krindle had been unable to accept it, could he ever have gotten the men aboard the ship to accept it? Who would accept it? He recognized the blindness of the instinct that had taken him toward Philadelphia, toward Patrice. The inexplicable had broken her. Perhaps an explanation would heal her. She would be anxious to be healed. She had accepted the world as a jungle, believing only in her own strength. When her strength had failed her, she had no other resource. Nothing else in which she believed.

The danger, he knew, was that "they" would anticipate his need to see Patrice, would be waiting for him. Though he recognized the danger, he knew at the same time that there was nothing personal in their attitude. Perhaps they had found that some people identified themselves so closely with the known world that even, after training, they were incapable of accepting an assignment that was —in essence—merely a wry and confusing game with no discernible purpose or rules. A children's game where all were blindfolded except the agents themselves.

As night came the streets of Philadelphia began to fill with the pleasure seekers. Electronics had played the rudest of all jokes on the people of the United States. By 1955 television had developed from an interesting drug into a vast obsession. Most children had had almost five years of it. It was not necessary to develop any resource of self-amusement, any intellectual curiosity. It was only necessary to sit and watch and be amused. The electronics industry met the vast challenge of millions of home sets, hundreds of stations. The war diverted the capacity of the electronics industry into military channels, and decimated technician personnel. One by one the stations began to fail, unable to replace essential parts. By hundreds, and then by thousands, the home sets became silent. After the war, amid economic exhaustion, there was a short period of resurgence, with stations re-activated, with home service available in meager amount. But it slowly tapered off again into the increasing silence. The triditoriums cornered the small capacity of the electronics industry. A few channels were still active in major cities, but there were no more networks. Just individual stations showing old films, over and over and over again.

In millions of front rooms there was a cubical object of polished wood and white lightless tube. But the resources of the individual to amuse himself without commercial assistance had been sadly weakened, weakened by the years of the glowing tube. So they went out onto the streets at night to escape the silent homes, to escape the doom of sitting in silence, with nothing to say to each other. There had to be some answer to boredom, and the answer became fleng and prono and tridi and violence. Ten-minute divorces and gangs of child thugs. Yet it couldn't be criticized too bravely or too loudly. Criticism was a Disservice to the State.

Telecast of India had made a survey to determine whether it was economically feasible to re-activate the industry in the United States. But with the breakdown of transportation, the decline of the technician class, the trend toward regional self-sufficiency, there were no longer commercial sponsors able to afford the high cost of network television. And Telecast of India was not concerned with any project which would fail to show a profit.

Dake walked tall and alone through the brawling night streets. Large areas of the city were in darkness again. He tried to telephone Patrice. It was a half hour before the call went through to the right number. He heard the distant ringing of her phone. He hung up after ten rings. At last he remembered the name of one of her lawyers, and found his home phone listing.

The lawyer was hesitant about giving her address. Dake identified himself as a Mr. Ronson from Acapulco, phoning about a hotel investment Miss Togelson had been considering.

"I suppose you could talk to her, Mr. Ronson. But she is taking no interest in business matters these days. We're handling her investments for her."

"She was very interested in this property."

"If she is still interested, we'd be very pleased. It's most difficult to please a client who . . . gives us no clue as to her wishes. She is at Glendon Farms, Mr. Ronson. It's a private convalescent home outside of Wilmington. But you won't be able to contact her tonight. Visiting hours are, I believe, in the afternoon."

Dake thanked him, hung up. He ate from a sense of duty, not hunger, and found a cheap hotel room. He lay on the bed in the darkened room and thought of his motives in trying to see Patrice. To find just one person who would accept, who would believe, who could be made to look at the shape of the enemy. . . .

To have suffered those incredible alterations was to become desolately lonely. He had never been particularly dependent on emotional attachments. But to have the certain knowledge that to human man he was an object of fear and dread, and to extra-human man a rebel to be immediately eliminated—it gave him a sense of apartness that shocked him, it was so unexpected. He knew that he could go down into the streets and find a woman and bring her back to this room. Yet any such intimacy would be a farce. A gesture as strangely indecent as those photographs showing a cat and a canary in precarious comradeship. He could go to a bar, and force himself into some group, and talk all night, without ever saying anything.

He knew, then, that the only true intimacy of the spirit was that intimacy possible only with those who had been trained as he had been trained. Only with those who had learned to focus and direct that incredible energy of the brain cells. With all untrained humans he would be a civilized man who had gone to live among savages. He could go native, but it would be a denial of his abilities. He would take to that savage tribe a knowledge of customs and abilities beyond their power to conceive, let along understand. And never would he be able to forget the thought of waste, of dispersal of power, of abnegation of destiny.

The closest friendship he had ever experienced had been with Watkins during the brief training period. In trust and friendship they had lowered screens, permitting an exchange of thought subject to no semantic distortion. It had been easier, more relaxing, to use speech rather than para-voice, but in any particularly difficult concept, where there was a misunderstanding, para-voice had been available. The thought changed itself into the words the listener would have used to express the exact shade of meaning.

Maybe, he thought, the agents are right. If a man could not accept the implications of training, he might be better off dead. Death could be no greater loneliness than this knowledge that you were forever cut off from other minds attuned to yours in a way that, once experienced, became forever necessary.

But he could not reconcile himself to defeat. The answer was clear. Make Patrice understand, and she would divert all her resources to the task of making the world see what was happening, what apparently had been happening for years without end. Perhaps untrained man could find a way to fight them, to keep them from toying like careless children with the destiny of man. But the first job was to expose.

He thought of the heads of swimming men, tiny against

the wide flat sea. He thought of those who would be waiting, in delicate awareness, for some indicative display of his new abilities, then using that detectable emanation to track him down, with an objective, functional mercilessness.

And he was honest enough with himself to wonder if he would have revolted against them if Karen had met him with the warmth he had expected of her.

CHAPTER FOURTEEN

A nurse with a heavy, placid face met him at the door of Patrice's cottage on the fenced grounds of Glendon Farms and took his visitor's card and asked him politely to follow her. Her starched uniform rustled, blinding white in the sunshine.

There was a long slope behind the cottage, down to a small formal garden. Patrice lay on a dark blue blanket spread on the tailored grass. She wore a brief black sunsuit.

The nurse paused with him, out of earshot, and said, "Please don't say anything to disturb or excite her. If you see her beginning to get nervous, call me. I'll wait here."

Dake walked down to her. Patrice was face down, her back deep gold in the sunlight. He sat on his heels beside the blanket and said, "Patrice?"

She turned quickly, raising herself on her elbows, a sheaf of the bright hair masking her eye for a moment before she threw it back with a toss of her head.

"Dake, darling," she said warmly. "How good to see you!"

"You look well, Patrice."

"I'm very well, dear."

He studied her curiously. There was something subtly wrong about her face, about her expression. A bland childishness. Her mouth and eyes were soft, but something had gone, utterly. He saw what it was. There was no firmness, no resolution, no strength of will or character left.

"Patrice," he said uneasily, "do you remember the . . . last time we saw each other?"

144

"That night when I got sick? They told me you were there, dear. Was I too awful?"

"No. I mean, you weren't really sick, Patrice. You just saw something you couldn't explain to yourself. But I could explain it to you."

She glanced up to where the nurse stood fifty feet away, guardian white against the green of the clipped grass.

She said in a low tone, "Don't let her know that I wasn't really sick. They're doing this for the money."

"What do you mean?"

She gave him a childish smile. "Don't be dull. If they find out I know what their little game is, they'll kill me. You certainly know that." Her voice was perfectly calm, matter-of-fact.

"What . . . do you plan to do?"

"Oh, there are too many of them! I can't do anything. You know that! But I have to let them all think I believe them. They give me warnings, you know. They put electricity in my head, and keep telling me it's going to help me, but it's just a warning about how they'll kill me if I don't do exactly what they say. Now you're in here and they won't let you out either. Because now you know, and you could tell about what they're doing. You were silly to come here, Dake, dear. Terribly silly. There are too many of them."

"Patrice, I . . ."

She sat up all the way and her voice became shrill, and her eyes were filled with sharp excitement. "Run, Dake! Run before the men come!"

The nurse came quickly down the lawn. Dake stood up and backed away from Patrice. The nurse said, "Now lie down and get some more sun, Patrice. That's a good girl."

Patrice smiled at her and stretched out obediently. She yawned and closed her eyes, said in a sleepy mumble, " 'Bye, Dake, darling."

He walked back to the cottage with the nurse. "How is she?"

The nurse shrugged. "She'll improve for a time, and then retrogress overnight. There seems to be something, some memory she won't face up to. She's had two full series of shock treatments. They seem to help for a time, but the effects aren't lasting. She's sweet, really. Mild and cooperative. We never have to use restraint, except when she realizes she's due for another shock treatment. She thinks she's some sort of a prisoner here. That isn't uncommon, you know."

"She always had such . . . enormous energy."

"She seems quite content to vegetate, sir. That is common, too. A complete avoiding of decisions, or the reasons for making any."

He went back to Philadelphia, back to the cheap room. Branson might have understood. He was gone. Patrice was gone. Oliver Krindle was gone. In a sense, Karen was gone.

He sat on the corner of the desk, lean ankles crossed, and tried to plot his future actions. "They" would be spread quite thin. There would be many places in the world, many places in this country, where he'd be out of range, free to work out some plan of what to do with the rest of his life.

Someone had to believe! Odd, how important that had become. He could not risk it with anyone he had known. It would have to be a stranger. Someone carefully selected. And the demonstration of his abilities would have to be carried on where the chance of detection was remote.

He walked in the city, looking at faces, looking into the eyes of strangers with an intentness that made them uneasy. His training had made faces more readable. He saw shallow concerns, and fear, and aimlessness. He walked long miles through the city. He found no one in whose stability he could believe. At dusk he walked out on the rusting mass of the Delaware River Bridge, wondering if all the cities would be like this, if there would not be a face in all the world to trust, instinctively.

The bridge lights were out and the girl was a vague gray shadow a dozen yards away. There was a pale hint of her face, and then she began to climb the parapet. He ran as quickly and silently as he could. She heard him and tried to move more quickly. He caught a thin wrist, pulled her firmly back and down to stand by him, his arm around her slim body. She stood very quietly, her head bowed, trembling slightly.

"Are you certain you want to do that?"

"Yes." It was a whisper, barely audible.

He took out a match, struck it, shielding it from the fitful wind, tilting her chin up calmly to study her face. It was a young face, haggard, frail, vulnerable. She turned away from him.

"I'll do it anyway," she said. "Sooner or later."

"The reason is good?"

"Of course."

"I won't try to question you about it. I'll accept that. Your reason is good. Do you have a name?"

"Mary."

"Suppose you were given a chance to do something . . . that might be constructive, and then be permitted, later, to destroy yourself. Would that interest you?"

"Constructive. That seems an odd word for you to use." Her voice was low, the inflection good, articulation crisp, clean.

"You would have to take it on faith. I can't explain, yet."

"Hold a light by your face. I want to look at you."

He lit another match. She looked up at him. "The heavy sorrow of all the world," she said softly.

"What do you mean?"

"In your face. In your eyes. I work . . . used to work, in wood and stone and clay, and anything else that will take a form." In the last dusk light he saw her hold her hands out, clench her fists. "Your face would fit a heroic figure. There aren't many faces left like that. It's a good face. Do you have a name?"

"Dake."

"I'll do what you want. But no questions. Will it take long?"

"A week, perhaps less. I don't know."

"I didn't know it would take that long."

"I have to tell you one thing, Mary. You have to be a person who . . . has very little to lose."

"I have one question. Is it something criminal?"

"No."

"All right. But first you better buy me something to eat. I'm pretty shaky."

In the small, lamp-lit restaurant he had his first chance to look at her. Her hair was straight, dark, worn long. She wore a gray suit, a white blouse, both of casual good quality, but rumpled. She wore no makeup. He sensed her lack of pretense and vanity. She had a style of her own, a directness. It was her hands that interested him most. Good square firm hands, with short, competent-looking fingers. They were as immaculate as a surgeon's.

She ate with controlled hunger, and with the precision of a starved house cat. He sat, smoking, and watched her.

At last he said, "I'm not asking questions about you. But in order to explain my position, I have to refer it to your customary frames of reference. Otherwise I might make myself meaningless to you. How do you . . . think about life, about the place of man in his environment?"

She made a face over her sip of substitute coffee. "Man," she said, "as a free spirit, has never had the freedom he deserves in his environment. He just drifts from one form of collectivism to the next. Taboos change—lack of freedom of expression is a constant."

"What causes his lack of freedom?"

She shrugged. "Ignorance, I suppose. Superstitions. The yen for the master-slave relationship. Or maybe plain bullheaded perversity. Let any person stand out as an individual, and the herd pulls him down and tramples him."

"Progress?"

"We wiggle back and forth in a groove, like a phonograph needle. On a flat surface."

"What if that's the plan?"

"Are you being a mystic?"

"No. Suppose it is an arbitrary plan, a definite supression, for an unknown reason?"

"Presumably, then, by some definite entity, some thinking aura of fire-ball or nine-legged Venusian?"

"By men who have been trained in . . . abilities you would think impossible."

She clapped her hands once. "What a lovely excuse for all defeatism! We can't possibly get anywhere because we're . . . breeding stock, or something. A rather poorly run stock farm, I might add."

"I have been trained on another planet."

She stared hard at him in a long silence. She picked up her spoon, put it down again. "This is where I should say I'm Mary, Queen of Scots, I suppose."

"If you'd like."

"They say madmen come in the most credible shapes and forms. I'm supposed to be mad, too. Suicidal. By the way, did you know the list of living creatures who do away with themselves? Lemmings, of course. That's common. And man, bless him. A scorpion, when infuriated beyond reason, will sting himself to death. And there is a species of white butterfly that flies straight out to sea. Those are the non-functional deaths, as opposed to the dying of, say, the male spider, or the winged ant. Yet . . . somehow I cannot believe that either of us is mad, Dake." She smiled and took a small glossy photograph from her pocket, slid it across the table to him.

He picked it up and looked at it. It was a photograph of a carving, in some dark wood, of a starving child. Spindle limbs, bloated belly, an expression of dull acceptance, without either pain or fear.

She said quietly, "I wasn't going to tell you. I planned not to. I've been working too hard. I've been doing too many things which . . . disturb my public. Apparently I've been critical. And criticism is a Disservice. Yesterday they came with a writ. They smashed my work. Every last bit of it. Hauled it away. Gave me an appointment with the Local Board for this afternoon. I didn't keep it. Suicide isn't a gesture of protest. Not in my case, Dake. It is very simply a statement. I refuse to permit myself to live in my environment. Am I mad?"

"I . . . don't think so."

"I'm not afraid of labor. I'm not afraid of being sentenced. You must believe that."

"I do."

She lifted her chin with a touching pride. "I've never been afraid of anything that walks, creeps or crawls."

"For myself, I would qualify that."

"How?"

"I've been frightened, but never afraid."

She tilted her head on one side. "I rather like that, Dake. Now what do you do with this training? Spread your filmy green wings and take off? Forgive me for sounding so flip. The food, I guess. Intoxicating after so long. I ate yesterday, before they came. That was the last time."

He leaned forward a bit. "You see, I have to make someone believe me."

"Or cease believing in it yourself? Maybe it's necessary for you to keep believing in it."

"That sounds like you're thinking of insanity again."

"Blame me?"

"No. But I want you to be . . . objective about proof."

"S art proving."

"I :an't. Not here. I can't even tell you why I can't do it hen . It will sound like a persecution complex running wild. f you're through, we'll leave. We're going to fly west."

"By flapping our arms? Oh, forgive me! I feel right on the ed_ke of tears or hysteria or something. Let's get out of here."

They sat in the deep comfortable seats of a CIJ flagship awaiting takeoff. Dake noticed that, under the terminal floods, the stairs had been wheeled back into position. Two men boarded the plane and came down the aisle toward them. Mary made a small sound, like a whimper. He saw the pale, flat, expressionless faces of Disservice agents, saw that they were staring at Mary, saw the eyes of the lead one widen as he glanced at Dake. A pink tongue flecked quickly at pale lips, and the hand slid inside the neat dark jacket.

He thought quickly. Takeoff was already seconds behind schedule. The Indian co-pilot glared at his watch.

Dake closed his hand over her thin wrist. "I have to demonstrate sooner than I wanted to," he said, barely moving his lips.

It would be too puzzling to the other passengers if the two men, whose profession was so obvious, should turn and leave the aircraft without a word. He selected a man across the aisle, an overdressed toothy man with a shyster look. He saw dullness replace alertness as he enfolded their minds in his will, thrusting volition aside ruthlessly. They turned, their movements awkward and poorly coordinated, and grasped the toothy man and hoisted him roughly out of the seat.

"Hey!" the man yelped. "Hey, what are you doing?"

Dake made them shove and thrust him up the aisle. He had to stand to see the wheeled steps. The struggling victim made the task difficult. The balance could not be maintained, and the three of them tumbled down the steps. The victim got up, was grasped again, and marched off toward the main terminal buildings, across the concrete apron.

The steps were wheeled away, the doors slammed and latched. The jets flared and roared, and quickly faded into silence as the flagship, turning above the city, arrowing upward, passed the sonic barrier. He realized he still had hold of Mary's wrist. He released it. She was looking up at him, her eyes unfrightened.

"They were coming after us, weren't they?"

"Yes."

"They wanted you too. I saw it in their eyes."

"Yes."

"You hypnotized them. I could see it in their walk. Such an odd walk. Will they . . . stay that way long?"

"As soon as they were out of range, they got over it."

"Won't they have the tower call the plane back?"

"I don't think so. They don't like to inconvenience CIJ in any way. And I know how their minds work. That man. I had to pick him quickly. They won't be able to explain what they did, or why. So they'll take particular pains to find some recent act of that man which can be classed as a Disservice. I'd be willing to bet that they'll report that you weren't on the plane. And they'll conveniently ignore having seen me. Any failure of a Disservice agent is in itself classed as a Disservice to the State, you know."

"Then we're safe?"

"From the Disservice agents. But not from . . . another group."

"Who are they?"

Do you believe me when I say I was trained on another planet?

"Yes, Dake, I——— How in the world did you do that?"

In this world but not of it, Mary.

"Hold my wrist again. Hold it tightly. Hurt me with your hand."

"Why?"

"I have to believe that I didn't go off that bridge. I have to believe that all this isn't happening in some . . . gray place between the last life and the next."

He held her wrist tightly, made her gasp with pain. She smiled. "That's better, a little."

"The other group . . . they are the people who have been trained in the same things. I think they control the world. I can't make myself believe in . . . their motives. I think they are evil. And apparently, the penalty for misplaced loyalty is death."

"Wasn't there a myth about a god who left Olympus, who preferred to live with man?"

"Men hate gods and fear them. I learned that quickly."

"I don't fear you. I don't hate you. There's just . . . a very definite awe. Can the others . . . find you?"

"They may be there when this plane lands. The first stop is Denver. So there isn't much time for us."

"What else can you do?"

"What did we do while we were waiting for the plane?"

She frowned. "Walked, talked."

"Did we?"

He took over her mind quickly. The life left her eyes.

Her hands rested flaccid in her lap. He gave her a better memory. He brought the memory up out of the good years. A great glittering ballroom, open to the sky, an orchestra, playing for the two of them. He dressed her in silver blue, a dress sheathed perfectly to the uncompromising perfection of her body. Music of Vienna, and a sky with too many stars, and the long dance as he looked down into her eyes.

After a time he released her. Her eyes focused on his with a slow fondness, and then she gave a little shudder and flushed.

"Lovely, Dake. But like dancing in a dream. Light, effortless. I always trample on my partner's feet."

"But it was real, Mary. You believe it happened. So it happened."

She nodded, solemn as a child. "It happened."

"Would you like more magic?"

"Much more. All there is."

"Look at your hands."

He had covered her fingers with great barbaric rings, with the emeralds and fire diamonds of illusion. She touched the stones.

"They . . . exist."

"Of course. But all magic isn't gay." He dissolved all the rings but one, an emerald. He turned it into a small green snake curled tightly around her finger, its head lifted, eyes unwinking, forked crimson tongue flickering.

She flinched violently and then held her hand steady, stared at it calmly. "Magic doesn't have to be gay. It has only to be . . . magic."

"Do you believe?"

"In legend, Dake, it was necessary for you to sell your soul to the devil to be able to do this."

"I refused to sell. That's why there is a forfeit I have to pay."

"The same forfeit I'm paying voluntarily. When you're through with me." She bit her lip and said, "I'm like a child with a new toy. I don't want it taken away from me.

Those two men back there—will they remember what happened?"

"Not what happened while I was controlling them. Just before and after."

"Would the crew of one of these liners admit they had made an unauthorized landing?"

"They . . . might not, but . . ."

"Can you control all the passengers?"

"Not at the same time. I can put them to sleep, one by one, and give them a strong suggestion to remain asleep. But I can't fly one of these things. I can't therefore control the man flying it."

"Could you make him believe he'd heard orders to land somewhere else, the way you made me believe in that . . . dance?"

He thought it over. "That might be done. It's a case of erasing the memory later, though."

There had once been a vast bomber base near Cheyenne Wells. One strip was kept lighted as an emergency strip. The flagship rolled to a stop. Sweat stood on Dake's forehead with the intensity of his effort, with the diversification of it. He got the doors open. It was a thirty-foot drop to the hard surface. All around them the passengers slept. Up forward the crew slept, heavily. They walked on their toes inside the plane, talked in whispers. Dake let the emergency ladder down, climbed down and held the bottom steady as Mary clambered down.

A light came bobbing and winking toward them. A heavy man in khaki came out of the shadows. "What goes on here?" he asked.

Dake wasted no time on him. He took him over with punishing abruptness, made him stand aside, his eyes glassy. He took Mary by the hand and they ran across the runway. He turned and looked back at the aircraft, at the lighted control room. The crew stirred, came awake, looked around.

Dake and Mary ran and hid in the grass, watchful. After a time the flagship wheeled ponderously around, raced down the runway, lifted toward the stars.

CHAPTER FIFTEEN

In the desert the nights were cool and dry, the days crisp, blinding. It was a miner's shack, abandoned when the claim was worked out. Mary drove into town eight miles away once a week for supplies. Fuel was a problem, water was a problem, money would soon be a problem. But each day was an idyll, each night pale silver with too many stars. They would sit on an outcropping of rock, still warm from the sun of the day. He would wonder where he had been—which exact portion of the big sky.

She wore jeans and white shirts and went barefoot gingerly until her slim feet were brown and toughened. The sun bleached the ends of her hair, whitened her brows and lashes, and turned her face a deep ruddy brown. He liked to watch her. She had a cat's grace, a cat's ability to relax utterly. They walked miles across the harsh burned land. They talked of all things under the sun.

Mary never tired of making him perform. The tiny Pack B fascinated her. He taught her the sequence of wheels, tried to teach her how to use it. She tried until she was on the edge of tears, saying, "I can't get rid of that last tiny little feeling that it's impossible. If I could only accept it completely. . . . Do it again, Dake. Let me watch again."

And finally she refused to try anymore. Her smile seemed a bit strained.

There was another game. She would say, "I met this one when I was studying in Sarasota right after Korea. About five foot six, a hundred and seventy pounds, I'd say. Balding, with very silky blond hair. Big bland blue eyes, and a snub nose and a puckery little mouth, and two chins. He stood very straight, with his stomach sticking

out, and when he was thinking of how he would explain
something, he'd suck his teeth. He used to wear white
slacks and a beaded belt and dark shirts with short sleeves,
navy or black."

"Like this?"

And she would clap her hands with sudden delight, or
she would frown and say, "He's wrong, somehow. Let me
think. It's the forehead."

And he would alter the illusion until she was satisfied,
and he would fix the man in his memory, ready to reproduce him at any time she desired. Once they had a party.
He produced the illusions of a round dozen of the people
she had described. He created them to the extent of his
abilities, sitting taut with the strain of managing so many
of them. And Mary walked among them, burlesquing the
considerate hostess, saying outrageous things to them.

And suddenly she began to laugh, and she sat down on
the sand, and laughter turned to tears, her face huddled
against her knees. He dissolved the illusions and went to
her, kneeling beside her, touching her shoulder.

"What is it?"

She lifted her wet face and tried to smile. "I . . . don't
know. It's a crazy thing. I started feeling as though I'm . . .
here with you like a favorite puppy, or an amusing kitten
or something. And what you were doing was like throwing
a ball for me to fetch it back to you, panting and wagging
my tail."

"Not like that."

"Dake, what are we doing here?"

"I had to have someone accept what I could do. Take it
without fear and without horror. It seemed necessary to
find someone, to find you."

"But I'm shut out, aren't I? I'm . . . like that puppy."

"How honest do you want me to be?"

She was solemn. "All the way, Dake."

"I have a feeling of guilt, about the things I can do and
you can't. Guilt makes me resent the fact that you can't.
I'm dissatisfied with your lack of ability."

"I'll be honest too. I envy you. And it's a very small
step from envy to resentment, from resentment to hate. I

keep saying to myself, 'Why did they take him? Why did they train him? Why wasn't it me?' Do you see?"

"Yes, I see, Mary. I've told you . . . every part of the story. Every part of my life, I guess. You know how it happened."

"I know how it happened. And I've watched you, Dake. I've watched you sitting, staring at nothing, that puzzled look on your face. You haven't told me the whole thing, have you?"

He sat back on his heels, picked up a handful of sun-hot sand, let it slide through his fingers. He said, "These weeks here . . . it's the first breathing space I've had. The first time to think. My mind goes around and around in a crazy circle and then always ends up flat against a paradox that I can't solve, can't see around. A featureless thing like a wall."

"I think I know what it is, Dake. You tell me."

He picked up more sand, tossed it aside irritably. "Just this. The mind and the spirit are perhaps . . . indivisible. On Training T, I was trained by humans, in an alien series of mental techniques. Their method of conquering space, this Pack B, the buildings and methods I saw—all those came from some alien technology far superior to anything on earth. But their greatest advances are in the realm of the brain, and its great unused power. If the mind and the spirit are—instead, I guess I should say the mind and the soul—if they are indivisible, I should think that any increment in the power to use the mind would presuppose a greater understanding of the human soul. And if that is true, why is the influence of the trained ones inimical to mankind? Greater knowledge should mean greater understanding. So why haven't they made of Earth a decent, safe, sane place to live. I know that with the powers I have, if I could be the only man on Earth with these powers, I could lead this planet into the greatest period of prosperity and peace it has ever seen. If I could do it, by crumbling away the rotten spots, reinforcing the good spots, why don't *they* do it? I certainly have no corner on good will. I saw the people trained at the same time I was. I saw them change. I saw an ignorant Spanish Gypsy girl change utterly from a person who functioned on the instinctual animal level to a person who began to have sound, sincere, abstract thoughts and concepts. I've labeled the entire operation as something evil. And I doubt whether my label is . . . accurate. I have the feeling of some chance slipping away from me."

"I've had that feeling for some time, Dake."

"Then what is the answer?"

"There has to be some answer that you haven't seen yet."

"Then why didn't they tell me the answer?"

"Maybe you had to decide it for yourself. Maybe they gave you enough clues."

He smiled crookedly. "Then I should keep thinking?"

"Of course. And if you find the answer, you should go back." She stood up, brushing the sand from herself. "Walk?"

"Sure."

"Make me a mirage, Dake."

"What kind?"

"On that hill. Something cool. Something inviting."

He made heavy old trees and black shade and a limpid fountain. She took his hand and they walked across the desert floor.

"Not a puppy," he said suddenly. "Something special. Something I need. Patrice had a portion of it, once. Karen had some of it. Even the Gypsy had some of it. I don't know how to tell you what it is. Strength and warmth. The strong people never seem to be warm enough. The warm people too often have wills like suet. My wife was . . . right. So are you. I love you."

"Scratch me behind the ear and throw a ball and I'll fetch."

"Stop that!"

"Don't you see? Remember what they told you when you were learning arithmetic? You can't add apples and oranges. You have to change the bottom halves of fractions before you can add them together. I can't become like you. You can't retrogress to me. I'll be around as long as you want me, but my attitude will be . . . sacrificial."

"That's a hell of a thing to say."

"I want you to realize your 'apartness.' You can't love a human except condescendingly. You want desperately for me to be able to insert my thoughts into your mind, as you can into mine. But I can't. So we'll never have the sort of communication that you depend on, that you have learned to depend upon. Without that, I'm just a warm, articulated doll. Press the right switch and I'll say, 'I love you, Dake.' Flat and metallic and mechanical. But I cannot ever say it . . . in your way."

"But you do?"

"Of course. Puppies have a traditional attachment to their masters. A revolting adoration."

In anger he walked rigidly ahead. He glanced back and she was standing quite still, watching him. He turned and climbed across brown rock.

Look out! Snake!

He caught the glint of sun on diamond coils and jumped wildly away, feeling the faint brush of blunt head and fangs against the leg of his trousers. It was a gigantic rattler, as big around as his upper arm. He moved warily away from it. It coiled, then turned slowly and slid, like oiled death, off into the raw brown rock.

It was only then, his heart still thudding, that he realized the implication of what had happened. He turned and looked at the girl, a hundred feet away. She stood with her chin up, her arms pressed tightly against her sides.

He walked slowly down toward her, faced her. Her expression told him nothing.

"That night on the bridge?"

"I was never far from you, Dake, from the moment you left Glendon Farms."

There was a sick taste in his throat. "So I'm an assignment. Is that it?"

"Yes. I should have risked shouting. I didn't think of it. Para-voice was quicker and . . . it saved you. I could only think of saving you."

"Will you explain . . . everything to me?"

"Let's go back."

They walked in silence to the shack. They sat on the ground in the intense desert shade, in the dry coolness.

He laughed flatly. "I must have been pretty amusing, showing you all my little tricks."

"Quite sweet, actually. A strain, though, not using my screens for so very long."

"That's a nice word. Sweet. And you were a sweet puppy, Mary."

"Get all the bitterness out of your system, Dake."

"And very amusing that the subject of your assignment fell in love with you."

"Are you through?"

"What is it all about?"

"You were studied very carefully. There's a paradox you don't know about. Those who barely manage to get through without cracking are the ones who are eventually the most valuable. Take the Gypsy. She withstood it easily. And she very probably will never go beyond Stage One. It is the borderline ones who eventually become the Stage Threes. You will be a Stage Three someday, Dake. I know I'll never go beyond Stage Two. So you see, you are rare and valuable."

"Thank you," he said, with irony.

"It was Karen's duty to start you running. She did it very neatly indeed. You weren't as much afraid of death as you were afraid of dying without ever knowing what Watkins called the ultimate answer."

"Why was I supposed to run?"

"Because there is an attitude which you will have to maintain for many years. It can't be superimposed on you, without limiting your effectiveness. It is a balance and a philosophy that you have to acquire by yourself. Only then are you ready for assignment. You have acquired a large measure of that philosophy here on the desert, with me."

"This philosophy has dimensions? Standard parts?"

"They vary for the individual, Dake. One of the primary attitudes, however, is an awareness and appreciation of 'apartness.' I think you have that. Man hates and fears deviation, and will destroy it if he can. Thus your relationship to man, in your role of induced mutation, must be in somewhat of the nature of parent to child."

"I've felt that. A . . . pity. A remoteness."

"You can achieve identification with only those of your children who can be induced to aspire to . . . adulthood. You are a true adult."

"With a pretty callous attitude toward the children?"

"There has to be a lot of attrition, a continual thinning of the ranks in order that others may grow."

"Why?"

"What would the answer to that question be?"

He thought for a moment. "Would it be Watkins' ultimate answer?"

"Yes."

"Where is he?"

"Running, as you have been. Maybe he is back by now. Running, not from the fear of death, but from the fear of never knowing."

"Can you tell me the answer?"

She looked at him for a long time. "I have to know if you're ready, Dake. I have to know if you can accept it. Take my hands."

They turned, facing each other. Her lips moved quietly, "Screens down, Dake."

He was utterly lost in her eyes. Gone. Taken into some warm place. Taken into secret depths of oneness, of togetherness, of warmth, that he had never imagined could exist. This was a closeness far beyond that which could ever be achieved by the body. This was a spiritual mating, a clinging and mingling of souls, a high, wild, hard emotional experience that was beyond space and time. . . .

Then he was aware that they were releasing each other, that they were separating slowly into separate entities.

"I've wanted that for so long," she said gently. Her voice trembled. Her eyes were brimming. "I knew it would be . . . right."

"Am . . . I ready?"

Her lips twisted. "Your ultimate answer will be anticlimax, Dake. Now."

"I think I sense that. Maybe the obvious is always an anticlimax."

She stood up lightly. "No, stay there. This is history, Dake. Human history. History of galactic man, and his adjustment to his environment, and his answer to decadence. There is more than a hundred thousand years of recorded history. Someday you will learn more of it. It is part of Stage Two training. The heart worlds grew and learned and warred on each other, and combined, and found peace, and added to themselves those other planets and star systems as they achieved cultural maturity. Each manlike cultural system made its own contributions to the whole. For the sake of simplicity, we shall call the entire unity Empire. Examine that word *manlike*. If I had a complete adjustment, I would not use that word. Physiological deviations are small throughout the galaxy. We are all men. You saw several varieties on Training T."

"Acting a bit . . . servile."

"Of course. One cultural group, part of the unity of Empire, is called the Senarian. It was that group which carried mathematical calculation to the inevitable pitch where it can make a sound prediction of the future. Perfection of extrapolation, the inevitable end result of all mathematical science. The parsing of time. Many thousand years ago the calculations of the Senarians were directed at a problem which was growing more serious. It had started in a very subtle way. It was noticed that, as new cultures were added to the unity of Empire, there followed a period when the top administrative jobs of Empire, the crucial decision-making positions, were all manned by citizens of the most recent culture to join Empire. After a few generations of the peace and sanity of membership in Empire, the descendants of the newest culture would lose their competitive drive, and no longer be of valid worth for leadership purposes. This was not a pressing problem so long as there were a sufficient number of barbaric cultures forging ahead toward Empire membership, as they would provide the future leadership, the future vitality which would avoid stagnation. But, the Senarians asked their vast computers, what will happen when there is no longer such a supply?

"The answer was disheartening to Empire. Leadership cannot come from any environment where there is peace and plenty. Leadership can only be developed in an environment where there is conflict, savagery, violence, hate. Leadership is the answer to a competitive environment. Empire is not a competitive environment. Empire will eventually be without leadership. Progress will cease.

"The computers were asked a second-level question. What will be the result of the cessation of progress? The answer was destruction. Destruction by life forms of neighboring galaxies. Life forms so alien that there could be no communication. Only through progress could there be a continual increment of strength sufficient to keep the species alive.

"A third question was asked. What can be done? The answer took much longer. And the logic of it was inevitable. Keep one planet in a barbaric state. Keep it in continual conflict. Permit it no knowledge of the existence of Empire, and no knowledge of its function. Do not permit it to destroy itself. Deny it any more than token space travel. Keep it in insane and continual conflict and that planet will provide you with your leadership. Take those men and women who rise to the top of the boiling pot, and skim them off, and train them, and use them."

He stared at her in the silence. "Then all this . . . all this that has tortured men for thousands of years . . . it is just a . . . trick? A breeding ground? A training ground?"

She looked at him proudly. "More than that, Dake. Much more than that. Earth is the heart of Empire. The ruler. The destiny of the galaxy. Men of Earth rule all the countless stars. They rule justly, firmly, ruthlessly. Under the leadership of Earth, Empire moves on up the infinite ladder of progress, up to a strength that will keep us free forever."

"Why was Earth selected?"

"Because here man was stronger than elsewhere. His natural environment had been harsher, gravity stronger

than the norm, climate more extreme, nature more vi-
olent."

"But I——"

"No more, Dake. Not now. You have to think over
what I've told you. You have to understand how you must
transfer your loyalty from Earth man to Galactic man. But
transfer it with an increment in pride in Earth, and in
yourself. I will talk to you later, after you have had a
chance to think it over."

CHAPTER SIXTEEN

He walked alone, and did not know where he walked, or how far. He stood on a hilltop and watched the sun slide red behind the far blue of the mountains. It made such a complete reversal of all his concepts, of all his adjustments to the political and emotional climate of his environment, that he felt as though someone had taken his brain between two hard hands, and twisted it like a sponge.

There was no segment of his beliefs that did not need reorganization, reevaluation.

Earth had a history. There were names in that history. Alexander, Hannibal, Napoleon, Hitler, Stalin, Mussolini. And, he thought, Christ. And Buddha and Muhammad and Vishnu. Good and evil, fighting an endless battle, to a predestined draw. Keep the pot boiling. Keep the four horsemen riding across the ravaged lands. A million men broken and burned and dying for each one selected. Massive, callous, mathematical cruelty, for the sake of . . . the greatest good for the greatest number.

He sat on the hilltop rocks and watched the stars come out, watched the quick desert night fall like a curtain. Men of Earth, being led in a crazy dance of death, for the sake of the high, wide ballroom of the skies.

He heard Mary's foot touch a loose stone. She came up behind him. He did not turn. He felt the soft warm pressure of her hand on his shoulder.

I know how difficult it is.

What is the final adjustment? What do I feel, afterward?

"Joy, Dake. Gladness. Pride. Humility. All the best attributes of the human spirit."

"Will you answer questions? I've been thinking in circles again."

"Of course."

"Why did I have to be sent back here?"

"Assignment here is part of your training for your future responsibilities. Part of your training in logic, in analysis, in action, and in humility. When your work is valid, you will be credited for it. After you have acquired enough credits, you will be given Stage Two training and returned here. Later, perhaps, you will be accepted for Stage Three training. After three tours here you will be assigned to the post in Empire that you are best qualified for."

"How long will I have to be here?"

"That depends on your progress. Twenty-five to thirty of their years."

"Their years?"

"Earth years. Two and a half to three of ours, basing it on effect of time."

"I want to gloat about that. And feel guilty. That's a very precious gift."

"But not mystic. Just one logical result of an advanced medical science. A continuation of the trend you've seen here on earth."

"Another question. There are two groups, apparently, or more. In conflict with each other. I don't see why that should be necessary, or even advisable."

"Is any untrained man a fair match for you?"

"N-No, but . . ."

"Did any man ever play a great game of chess, alone?"

"No."

"Conflict breeds ingenuity. Competition, also, gives a more random result, one that is less predictable, less likely to be detected by the ordinary thinking man as the result of extra-terrestrial interference. You get credit for accomplishment, and you pay, as Karen did, a penalty for failure. And always you must watch. You watch the top people in every possible line of endeavor. The most successful crooks, as Miguel Larner was. The best statesmen, the best politicians, the best artists, designers, salesmen, engineers. People at the top of every heap got there through conflict, through a compensation for some type of psychic trauma. If the incomprehensible doesn't drive them mad, they become our best recruits."

"Why wasn't Darwin Branson recruited? He was killed, wasn't he?"

"He had an organic disorder that was too far advanced for treatment. It would have killed him within six months. Besides, it was only during the last three years of his life that he achieved more than a pedestrian impact on his environment. So he wasn't noticed until too late."

Dake absorbed that in silence. He stirred restlessly. She sat on the rocks beside him.

"There are so many loyalties to give up," he said. "Loyalty to my country. That was pretty strong, you know. And now I can see that its weakness is due to what . . . we have done to it."

"That word was good to hear. We. It's an acceptance. Here is something you should consider. The number of recruits we obtain from any one country is in direct ratio to the extent of hardship that country is undergoing. During India's years of poverty and exploitation and death we obtained many recruits there. During the fattest years of the United States it was difficult to find people sufficiently toughened, hardened. Sword steel is treated in flame. Civilizations rise and fall. Those on top are poor breeding grounds for leadership. See, you have to reverse all your concepts, Dake. Good becomes weakness. Evil becomes strength."

"And isn't it all a vast rationalization?"

"So is the life form itself. A rationalization of the means of survival."

They walked back to the shack, walking in the starlight that silvered the sand underfoot. A coyote cried far away, cried of unmentionable woes and wrongs. He felt the girl shiver.

"We'll start back in the morning," he said quietly.

"In the morning, Dake."

They stood for a time and watched the stars, near the dark hulk of the shack. He held her hand, felt her mind

touch gently at his. They stood again in the climactic oneness, and later he began to feel the first faint stirrings of
dedication, the first wary reachings toward a philosophy
that would have to support him, amid cruelty, for long
years of service to a barely comprehensible dream.

CHAPTER SEVENTEEN

The cabdriver was sweaty, irritable, and talkative.

"Guess you folks have been out west. I can tell by that tan. You don't get that kind of tan here in summer, or in Florida, or anywhere except out there. Jesus, it's been a hot August here. Wet. I wish to hell I was back out where it's dry heat."

"It's more comfortable," Mary said.

"You bet your elbow it is, lady. This town goes nuts in the summer. All the rummies start sleeping in the parks. Bunch of pronies running around cutting up people. Another fleng joint war, with them throwing bombs in each other's joints. Gawd, what a month. You hear the knock in this thing? I'm running it on kerosene, and damn poor kerosene at that."

The driver cursed and swerved wildly to avoid a big Taj full of Pak-Indian tourists. "Think they own the damn world," he said viciously. He shrugged, arguing with himself. "Maybe they do, come to think of it."

"Have there been many tourists around this summer?" Dake asked.

"Too many, if you ask me. I don't know why they come over here. I got a pal with connections. He's all lined up to emigrate. Going to run a hack in Bombay, with a Sikh partner. He's never had it so good. They got those quotas so tight, it's almost impossible to get in over there."

"You'd like to do the same thing?"

The man turned in the seat and gave him an angry glare. "Why the hell not? What is there here? Three days a week I get fuel. I get four deadheads for every tipper. I don't even own this hack. Where's the opportunities here?

I ask you that. When I was a kid it was different. My old man owned six cabs. He had it nice. All the gas he could use." He stopped for a light and turned around and gave Dake a puzzled stare. "What happened to us? You ever try to figure that out? Where did it all go?"

"The war."

"That's what everybody says. I wonder. Seems like soon as we start to climb up there again, we get knocked down. Something always tripping us up. Somebody always tripping the whole world up."

"And then picking it up again?" Mary asked, smiling.

"Lady, in this world, you pick yourself up." He started up slowly, cursing the cars that passed him. "You know what I figure?"

"What?" Mary asked obediently.

"I figure we got to depend on those atom rocket boys. They're working day and night, I understand. What we haven't got is resources. Now you take Mars, or Venus. I bet those places are loaded with coal and oil and iron and copper and every damn thing we need. We just got to get there first and stake a claim. Then we'll be okay."

"And if we never get off the Earth?"

The driver's shoulders slumped. He said, in a dejected voice, "You know, mister, I just don't like to think about that. It means we're stuck here. And things aren't the way they used to be. My old man used to take me out to Yankee Stadium. Yell his fool self hoarse. Can I do that? Who wants to yell at a bunch of silly broads playing softball, I ask you? Those good old days, mister, they're gone. Believe me. TV we had, and baseball, and all the gas you wanted. Every time I see those Indians around, I feel like maybe we're one of those kind of tribes, with bones sticking through our nose, and big spears. We're for kicks, mister."

They rode in silence for a time, nearing the apartment. The driver said, "When we used to have all them saucers around, my old man used to say it was time the Martians landed and took over. The old man had something, you know. Know what I think?"

"What?" said Dake.

"I figure those Martians took a good long look around and said to each other, boys, we better go away and come back in ten thousand years and see if these folks have grown up any. Man, it's dangerous down there. Is this place you want in the middle of the block?"

"Right over there on the right, driver," Mary said.

"Class, eh? Isn't that where that racketeer used to live? Larner? Mig Larner?"

"That's the place, driver."

They got out. The driver took the fare, grinned. "I didn't figure you to deadhead me. I can almost always tell. Be good now. Watch out for them Martians."

They walked into the coolness of the air-conditioned lobby. Johnny came around from behind the desk, hand outstretched. "Here for good this time, Dake?"

"I think so."

"Little stubborn, was he, Mary?"

"Did I take long?"

"Last ones in, dear. Martin Merman suddenly became interested in your space requirements the other day."

Mary smiled. "He's a hideous person. What he doesn't know, he can guess."

Johnny went back around to his side of the desk. "Both of you in suite 8C then?"

Stop blushing furiously, darling.

"Yes, Johnny," she said.

"And so he'll twin you on assignments. You'll make an ominous pair, kids. Shard will have a happy time assigning the equivalent. Now Martin is expecting you for a couple of brief impressive ceremonies."

They went down to the dioramic garden where Dake had first met Miguel Larner. Merman got up, his young-old face smiling, his handshake warm and firm.

He said, "It isn't something we can give you, Dake. It's something you have to find for yourself. You found it with Mary's help. Are you ready to accept?"

"Completely."

"That's the only way we can . . . accept your acceptance. Without reservation. Raise your right hand, please. It isn't necessary to repeat the phrases after me. Just say 'I do' when I have finished. Do you, Dake Lorin, agree in heart, mind, and spirit with the eternal obligation of Earth, the planet of your origin, to provide leadership for Empire? Do you agree to accept dutifully all agent assignments given you with the full knowledge of the end purpose of those assignments, to provide leadership through keeping Earth, the planet of your origin, in a savage and backward state, where neither progress nor regression is possible? Do you promise to bring to this duty every resource of your mind and spirit, not only those resources recently acquired, but those developed in you by your environment prior to your association with us?"

Martin Merman's eyes were level, sober, serious.

"I do," Dake said.

"For the sake of all mankind," Martin Merman said.

"For the sake of all mankind," Mary repeated softly.

"Now you are one of us, Dake. I'll break your heart a hundred times a year, from now on. At times you'll be sickened, angry, resentful. You will be called on to do things which, in your previous existence, you would have considered loathsome. But you'll do them. Because the purpose is clear. Cold. Inevitable." He grinned suddenly. It was an astonishingly boyish grin. "Anything else, Mary?" he asked.

"Another . . . little ceremony, Martin."

Now who looks like a beet?

"This is a tribal ceremony, Dake," Martin said. "A uniting. It has no legal status among us. Only a moral and emotional status. Either of you can dissolve it at any time by merely stating the desire that it be dissolved. However, in our history, no such a uniting has ever been dissolved. It is, to pun badly, a mating of the minds. And in that field there can be no deceit, no unfortunate misunderstandings, no secrets, each from the other. You will live and work together as the closest possible team. You will complement each other's efficiencies, and heal each other's distress. Any children you may have will be taken from you and raised on one of the heart worlds, and you will renew your relationship with them once your duties here are over. They will still be children, still need you. And your eventual Empire assignment will be as close as your assignment here. Do you accept that?"

"If Mary does."

Mary nodded. Martin said, "Then we must have witnesses." He smiled.

There was the faintest shimmer and Karen suddenly appeared near them. And then Johnny. And Watkins. And one by one, others from his training class. And the persons he had seen in the lobby that night long ago. And strangers. Many of them. All appearing, grouping themselves in the bright garden, their faces reflected in the garden pool.

Dake had always been a lonely man. He had never been a part of a group, never relished it, except during the months on Training T. There, for the first time, he had experienced the vague beginnings of group warmth and group unity.

And the warmth of all these people suddenly surrounded him, enfolded him. They had proud faces, and level eyes, and something unmistakably godlike about them. Super-beings who walked among men with sadness, with pride, with humility.

That group identity caught him up. He was a part of it. He knew that never again would he have the feeling of walking alone.

He stood for long moments, tasting this final acceptance, sensing the challenge of the years ahead, knowing that at this moment he began his apprenticeship.

He reached and took Mary's firm brown hand, and turned just enough so that the two of them stood, side by side, facing Martin Merman. Her fingers tightened on his.

Dake Lorin squared his shoulders and stood quietly, awaiting Martin Merman's words.

AFTERWORD

I wrote *Wine of the Dreamers* in 1950 and *Ballroom
of the Skies* the following year.

When Knox Burger, who edits my work at Fawcett
Publications, suggested we resurrect these two books,
the only science fiction novels I have ever published,
I read them for the first time since the obligatory
reading in galley proofs nearly twenty years ago.

It would be a meretricious idiocy for any writer with
any respect and consideration for his following to
foist upon them the creative mistakes of the early years.
I have closets full of previously published stories
which will never see print again, regardless of
whether I am on the scene or off in that limbo which
I suspect is reserved for all novelists—where we are
condemned to live for half of eternity in tiny rooms
with the creatures of our own devising.

Though it may be merely one more symptom of the
writer's flawed objectivity, I found both these novels
to be more cohesive and provocative than
I had expected.

I have not revised them. I ached to doctor much
stilted conversation, but to do so would have been to
cheat, as somehow the pretentious and overly
grammatic speeches made by the actors are touchingly
typical of the genre.

They are both more accurately categorized as
science fantasy than as science fiction, in that they

are neither space-adventure, nor mad-scientist,
nor doom-machine epics.

The two novels are companion pieces in that they
provide two congruent methods of accounting for all the
random madness and unmotivated violence in our
known world, and two quite different answers as to why,
with all our technology, we seem unable to move a
fraction of an inch toward bettering the human
condition and making of life a universally more
rewarding experience.

This, for the writer, is the charm of such novels,
as they enable him to step up onto a small shaky
soapbox and say something, without ever lecturing the
reader, about the moral and emotional furniture of
our lives. Books of this sort have a functional
relationship to the world's religions, in that they also
make a sober attempt to explain the inexplicable,
account for the unaccountable.

I confess to being particularly jolted by finding in
Wine of the Dreamers that the Paris Peace Talks were
still going on in 1975, that the Asians were quarreling
with Russia about the orbits for snooper satellites,
and that a substance was being advertised and sold to
millions of Americans as a non-alcoholic, non-
habit-forming beverage which would heighten the
sensory response to such stimuli as a kiss or a
sunset. I wish I could have equivalent prescience in
personal matters.

To those of my reader-friends who are turned off
completely by these organized speculations and term
them "silly," I extend apologies. I am glad to have
these back in print. I suspect, however, that those
who cruise vicariously aboard *The Busted Flush* with
one T. McGee—as do I—will find things in these books
which will reward and amuse.

Herein there are no bug-eyed monsters, except the
ones forever resident in the human heart. There are

no lovelies being rescued by space explorers from giant
insects who talk in clicks and carry disintegrators.
No methane atmospheres. Nothing emerging from the
evil swamps. Not even a single dutiful robot, harboring
either electronic love or the cross-wired circuitry
of rebellion. Because of these omissions I may well
be responsible, also, for turning off the hard-core
aficionado of science fiction who, because these are
more about people than things, might also term
them "silly."

My most signal satisfaction in rereading these two
novels and in authorizing their reappearance was to
discover that I had not, as I had suspected, sacrificed
story to message. They move right along. It had
been so long since I had written them that my recall
was fogged by fifty intervening novels. And so I had
much ironic amusement in finding myself, for
the first time, reading my own work with
considerable curiosity as to what would happen next.

JOHN D. MACDONALD

Sarasota, Florida
September 1968